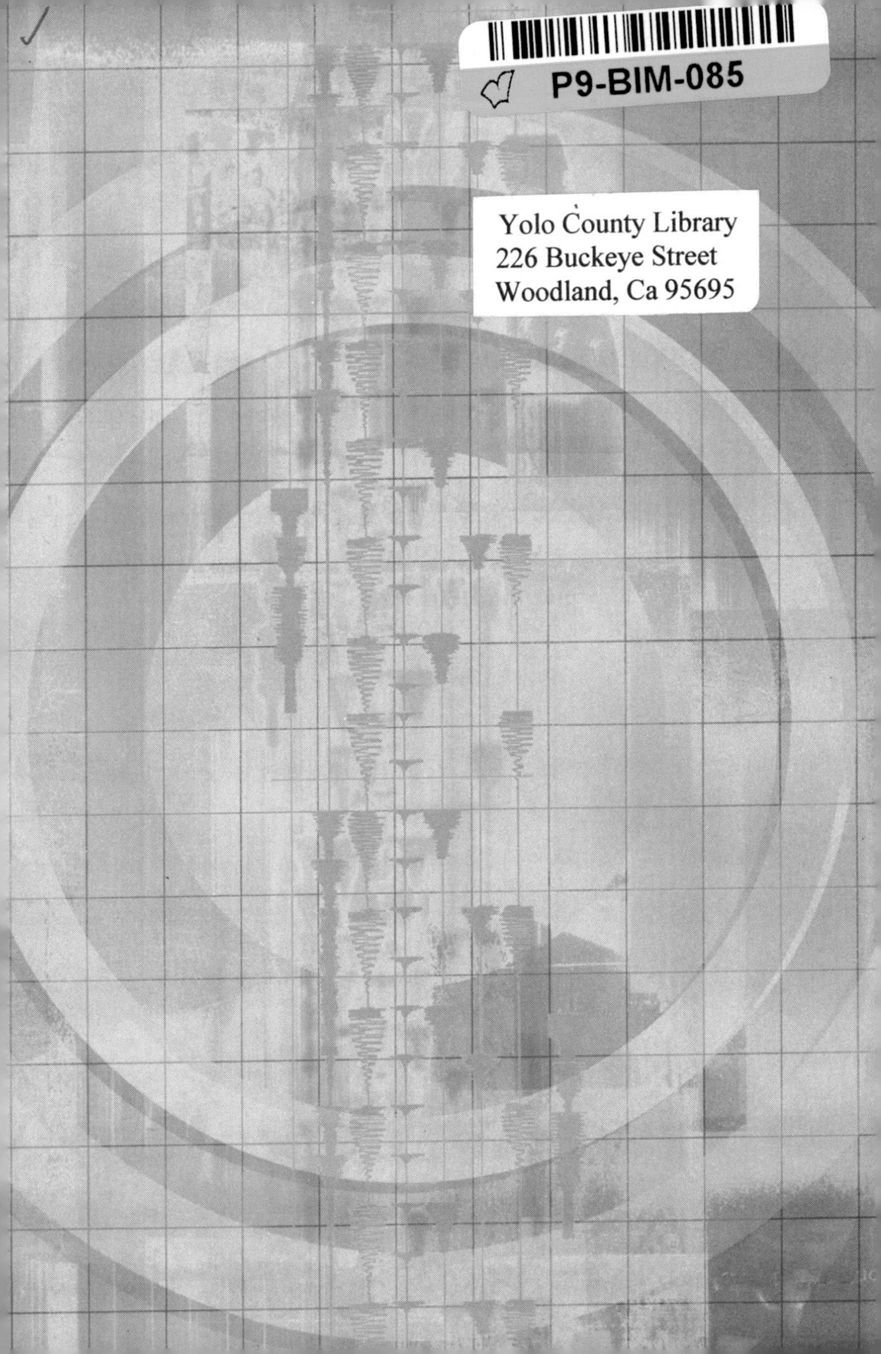

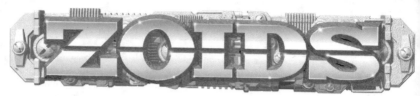

ZOIDS

Chaotic Century
Volume 08

Story and Art by **MICHIRO UEYAMA**

English Adaptation & Editing: William Flanagan
Translator: Kaori Kawakubo Inoue
Touch-up & Lettering: Dan Nakrosis
Graphics Assist: Carolina Ugalde
Graphics, Design & Zoids Guru: Benjamin Wright

Managing Editor: Annette Roman
VP of Sales & Marketing: Rick Bauer
VP of Editorial: Hyoe Narita
Publisher: Seiji Horibuchi

© Michiro Ueyama/Shogakukan
© 1983-1999 TOMY

First published in Japan by Shogakukan, Inc. as "Kiju Shinseiki Zoido." All rights reserved.
New and adapted artwork and text © 2002 Viz Communications, Inc. All rights reserved.

The stories, characters and incidents mentioned in this publication are entirely fictional.
For the purposes of publication in English, the artwork in this publication is generally printed in reverse from the original Japanese version.

Printed in Canada.

Published by Viz Comics
P.O. Box 77010 • San Francisco, CA 94107

10 9 8 7 6 5 4 3 2 1
First printing, September 2002

WHY IS IT BACKWARDS?
ZOIDS was originally a Japanese comic (manga), and since the Japanese read right-to-left, the comic you're reading is a mirror image of the original drawings. So if you noticed that the mark on Van's face is on the wrong side, that's why.

www.viz.com
• get your own vizmail.net email account
• register for the weekly email newsletter
• sign up for VIZ INternet

j-p☻p.com
www.j-pop.com

ZOIDS

Chaotic Century

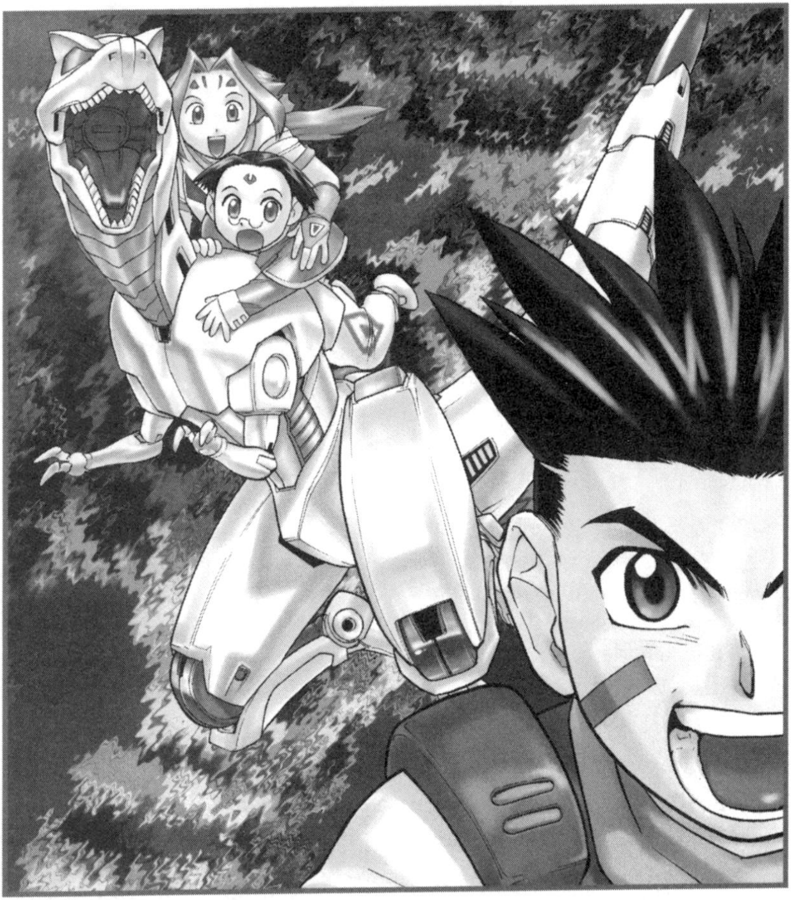

Story and Art by

MICHIRO UEYAMA

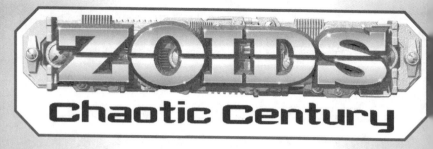

ZOIDS
Chaotic Century

Planet Zi orbits a sun sixty-thousand light years from our Earth on the opposite side of galactic center. There, countless varieties of giant life forms with metal-based bodies—ZOIDS—inhabit the world. The people of Zi took those lifeforms and altered them into beastly fighting machines, and the wars spread throughout the planet. When humans from Earth arrived in an enormous life-ship, they added their advanced technology to the war-like atmosphere causing a ZOID arms race.

Some 40 years ago, a gigantic meteorite collided with Zi. Millions were killed and a large portion of a continent was sunk beneath the waves. The strike caused cataclysmic earthquakes and volcanic eruptions—much of Zi's history was buried beneath lava and dust. Now, in the remote region of the Elemia Desert, young Van finds a small dinosaur-type ZOID and a mysterious young girl while searching a ruin. The ZOID, Zeke, can merge with Van and also merge with other ZOIDS, boosting their power and combat abilities. The girl remembers that her name is Fiona, but nothing beyond that.

Van, Zeke, and Fiona have joined up with the Shield Liger Caesar and set out on a journey looking for adventure and clues to the mystery behind the ominous words, "ZOID-Eve." In their travels, they team up with the cheerful saleswoman Moonbay who pilots her Gustav ZOID and rogue ZOID pilot Irvine and his Venomous Viper Tornado. Van and his friends have hitched a ride on the transport ZOID Kracken on their way to the capital of the Helic Republic to find more information about ZOID-EVE. On the way, they are joined by the young scientist Melissa Su who is trying to capture a rouge underwater ZOID, Viking, that is attacking all shipping! Little do Van and his friends know what dangers lie beneath the waves.

CAST OF CHARACTERS

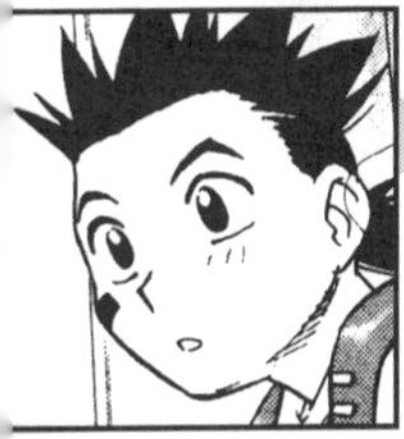

Van

A young man who is striving to be the best ZOID pilot there ever was!

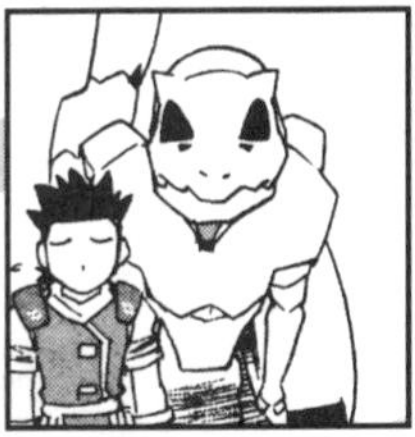

Zeke

An Organoid—a ZOID that can merge with other ZOIDS—and Van's best friend.

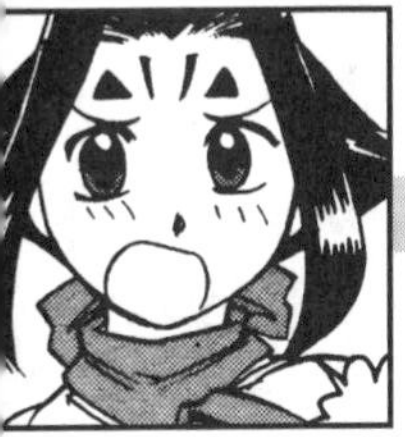

Fiona

A mysterious girl with a strange connection to ZOIDS.

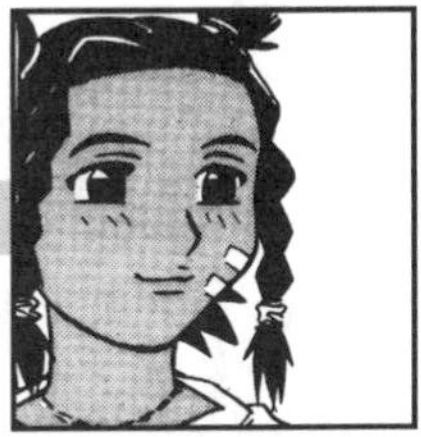

Moonbay

A helpful, enthusiastic merchant.

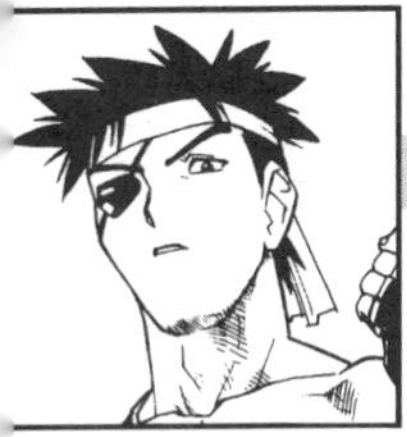

Irvine

A hard-bitten, cynical pilot of a Venomous Viper.

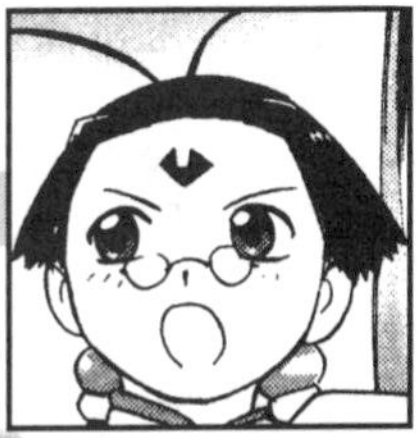

Melissa Sue

A very young scientist who is trying to track a rouge ZOID.

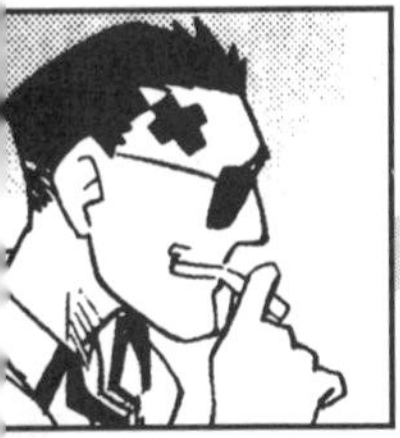

Prace

A top Empire spy.

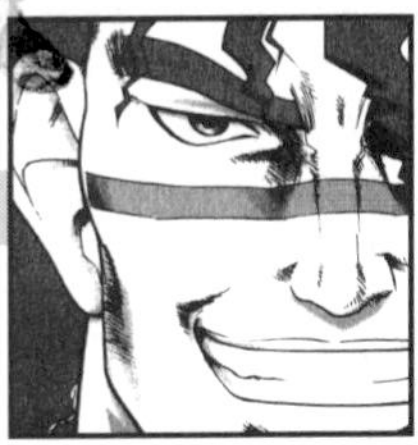

Rosso

A bandit leader of a group of military deserters.

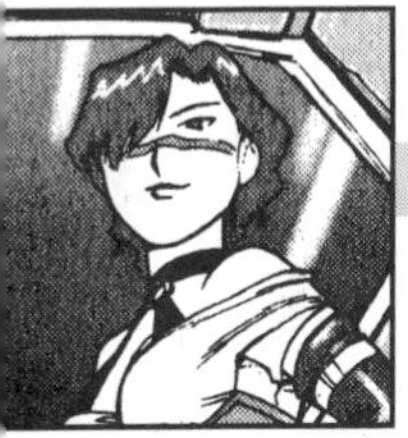

Viola

One of Rosso's top bandits.

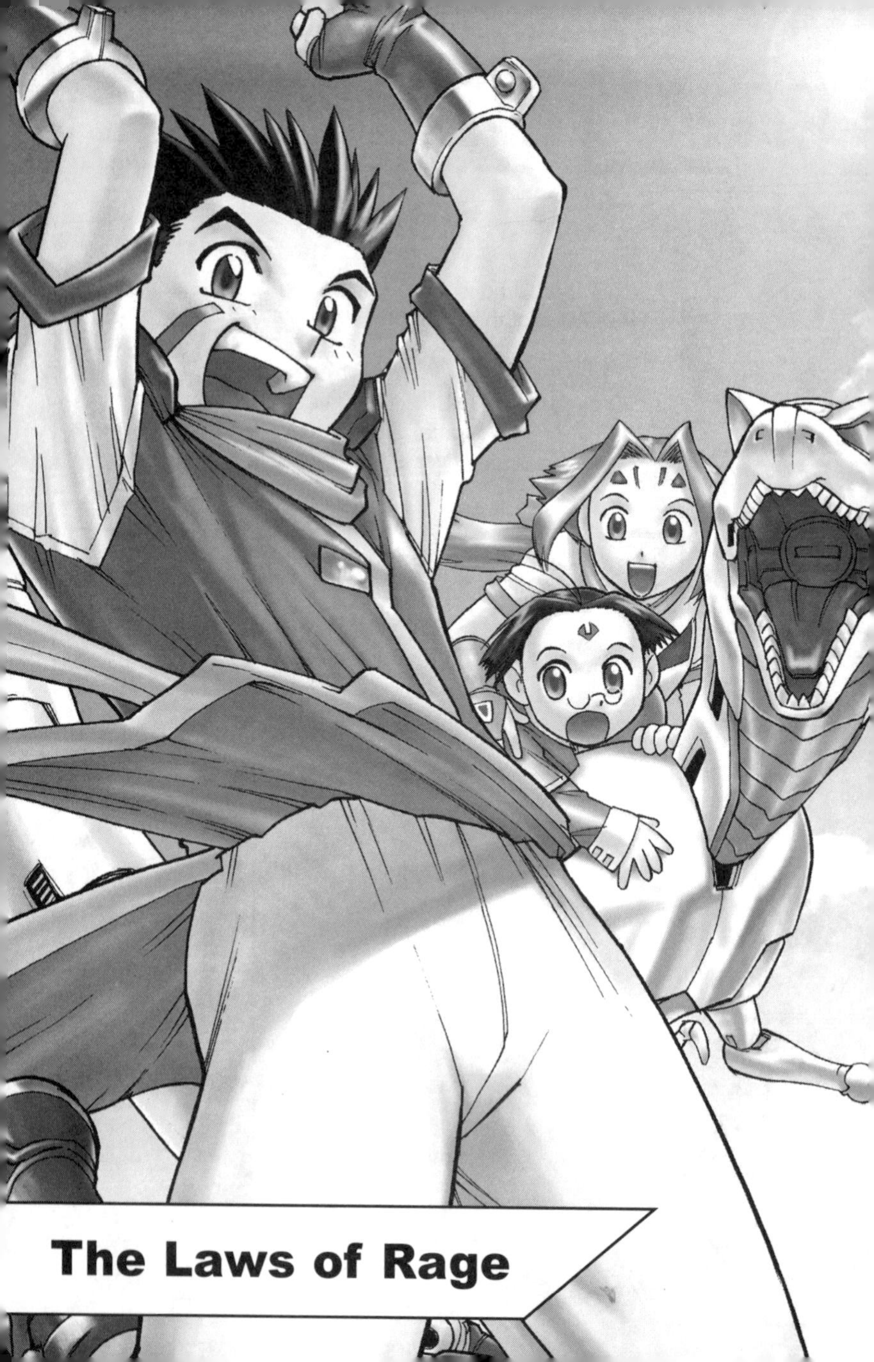

The Laws of Rage

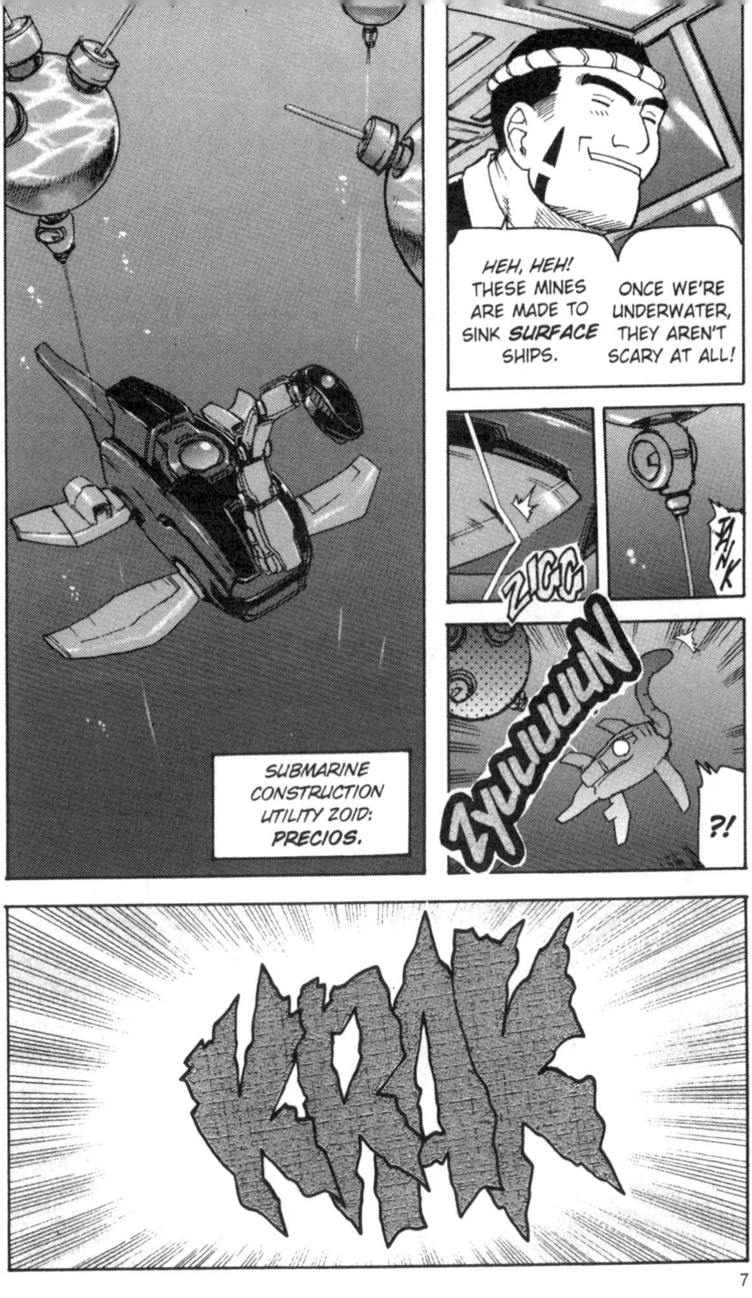
SUBMARINE CONSTRUCTION UTILITY ZOID: PRECIOS.
HEH, HEH! THESE MINES ARE MADE TO SINK SURFACE SHIPS.
ONCE WE'RE UNDERWATER, THEY AREN'T SCARY AT ALL!
ZICC
TANK
ZYUUUUN
?!
KRAK

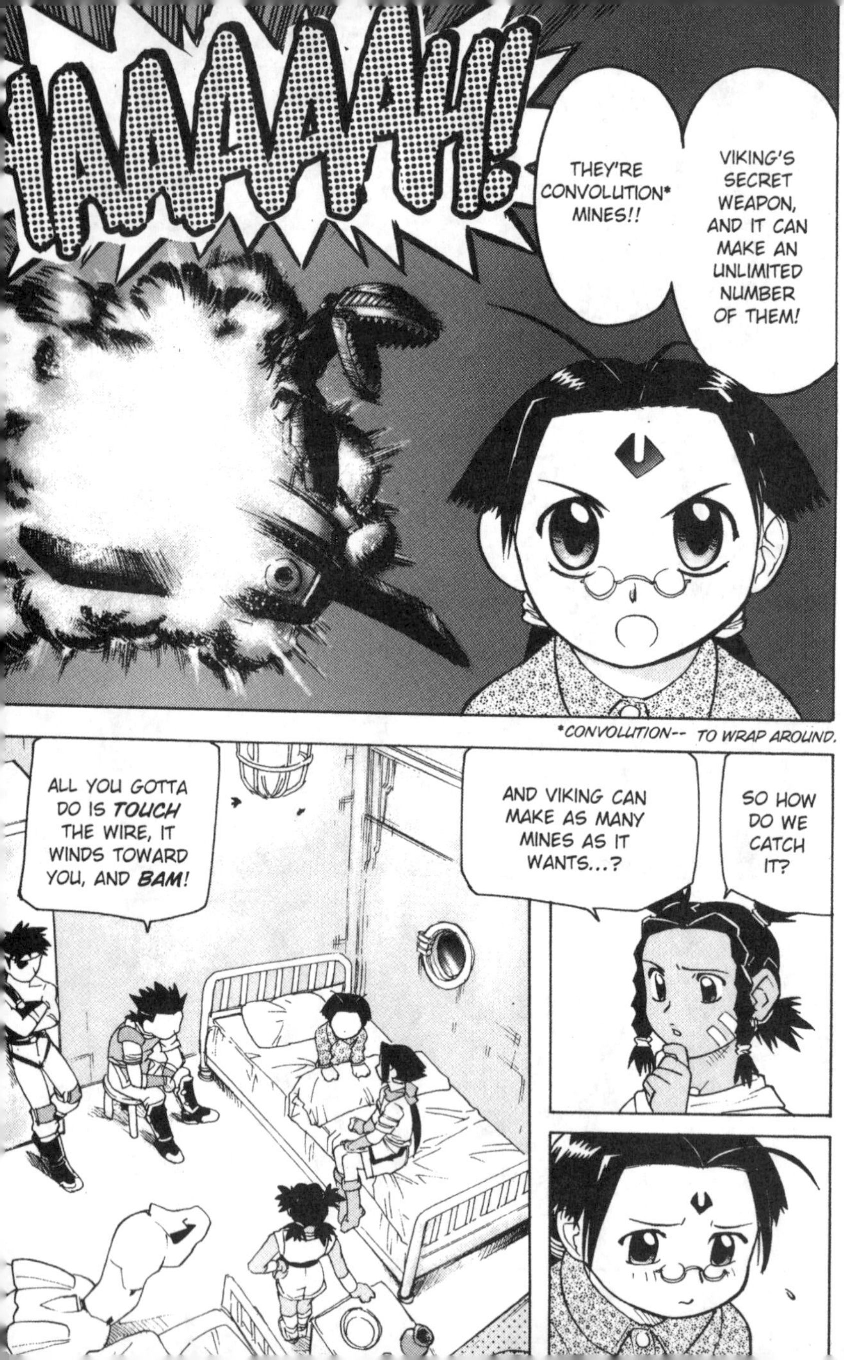
WAAAH!
VIKING'S SECRET WEAPON, AND IT CAN MAKE AN UNLIMITED NUMBER OF THEM!
THEY'RE CONVOLUTION* MINES!!
*CONVOLUTION-- TO WRAP AROUND.
SO HOW DO WE CATCH IT?
AND VIKING CAN MAKE AS MANY MINES AS IT WANTS...?
ALL YOU GOTTA DO IS *TOUCH* THE WIRE, IT WINDS TOWARD YOU, AND *BAM*!

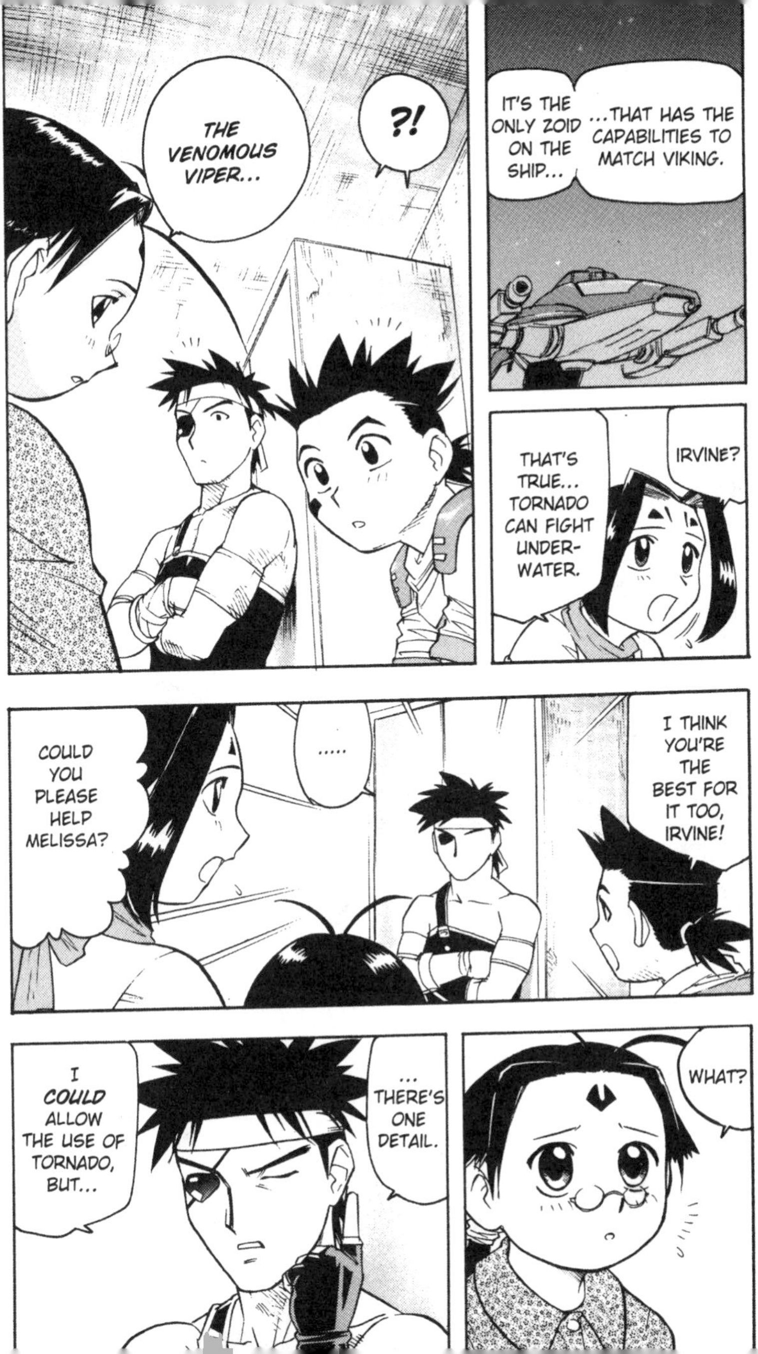
THE VENOMOUS VIPER...
?!
IT'S THE ONLY ZOID ON THE SHIP...
...THAT HAS THE CAPABILITIES TO MATCH VIKING.
THAT'S TRUE... TORNADO CAN FIGHT UNDER-WATER.
IRVINE?
COULD YOU PLEASE HELP MELISSA?
.....
I THINK YOU'RE THE BEST FOR IT TOO, IRVINE!
I *COULD* ALLOW THE USE OF TORNADO, BUT...
...THERE'S ONE DETAIL.
WHAT?

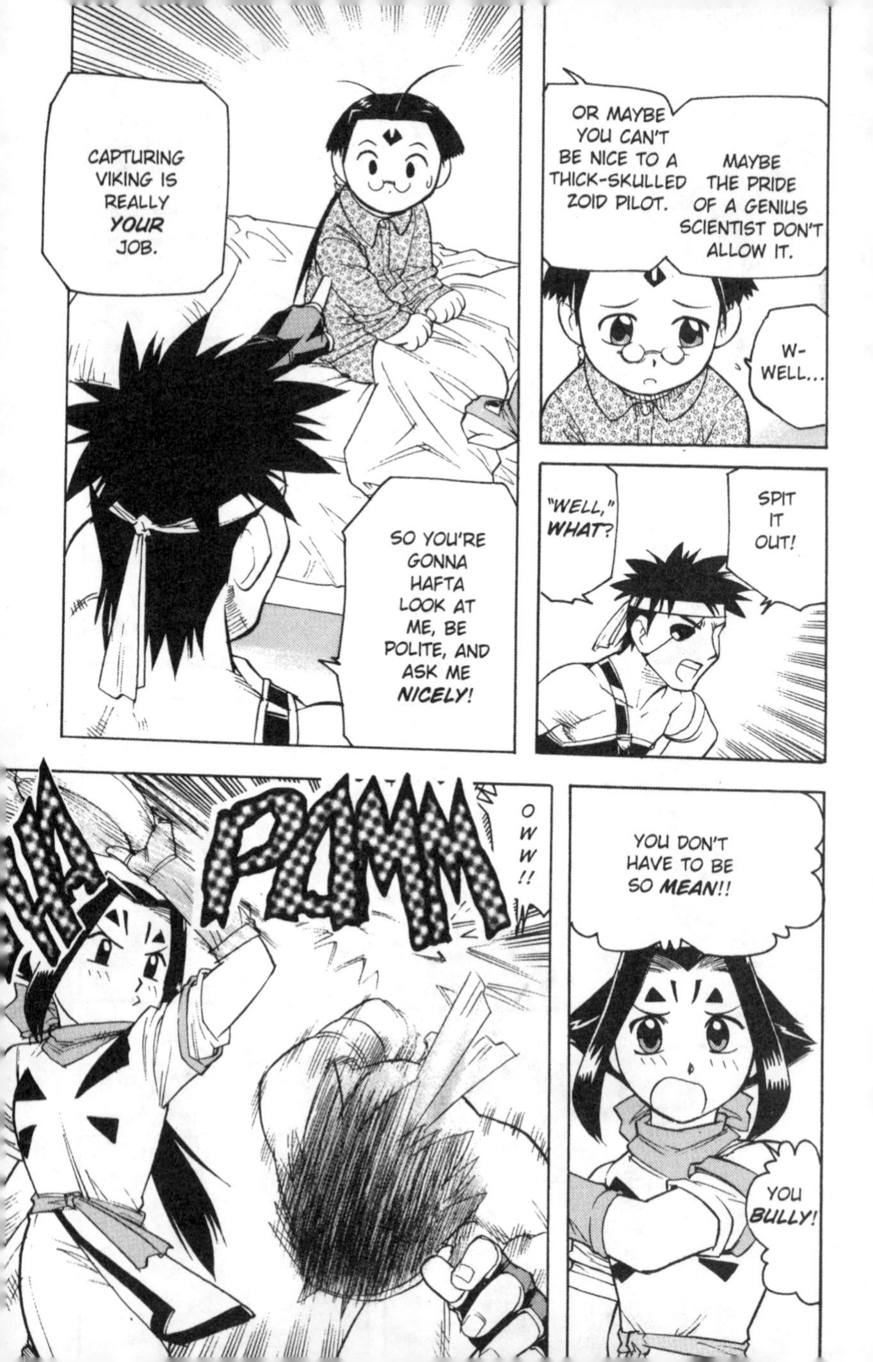
CAPTURING VIKING IS REALLY ***YOUR*** JOB.
SO YOU'RE GONNA HAFTA LOOK AT ME, BE POLITE, AND ASK ME ***NICELY***!
OR MAYBE YOU CAN'T BE NICE TO A THICK-SKULLED ZOID PILOT.
MAYBE THE PRIDE OF A GENIUS SCIENTIST DON'T ALLOW IT.
W-WELL...
"WELL," WHAT?
SPIT IT OUT!
OWW!!
YOU DON'T HAVE TO BE SO ***MEAN***!!
YOU ***BULLY***!

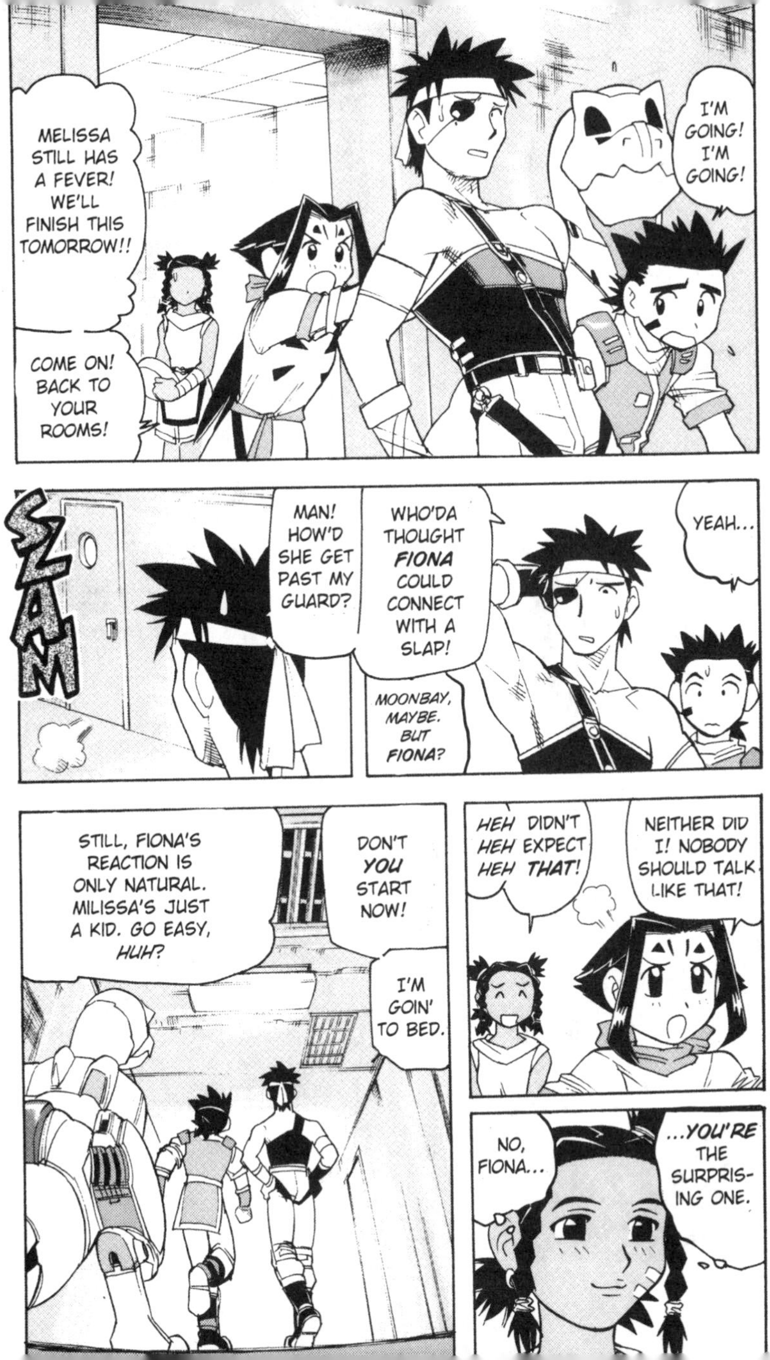
MELISSA STILL HAS A FEVER! WE'LL FINISH THIS TOMORROW!!
COME ON! BACK TO YOUR ROOMS!
I'M GOING! I'M GOING!
SLAM
MAN! HOW'D SHE GET PAST MY GUARD?
WHO'DA THOUGHT FIONA COULD CONNECT WITH A SLAP!
MOONBAY, MAYBE. BUT FIONA?
YEAH...
STILL, FIONA'S REACTION IS ONLY NATURAL. MILISSA'S JUST A KID. GO EASY, HUH?
DON'T YOU START NOW!
I'M GOIN' TO BED.
HEH HEH HEH DIDN'T EXPECT THAT!
NEITHER DID I! NOBODY SHOULD TALK LIKE THAT!
NO, FIONA...
...YOU'RE THE SURPRISING ONE.

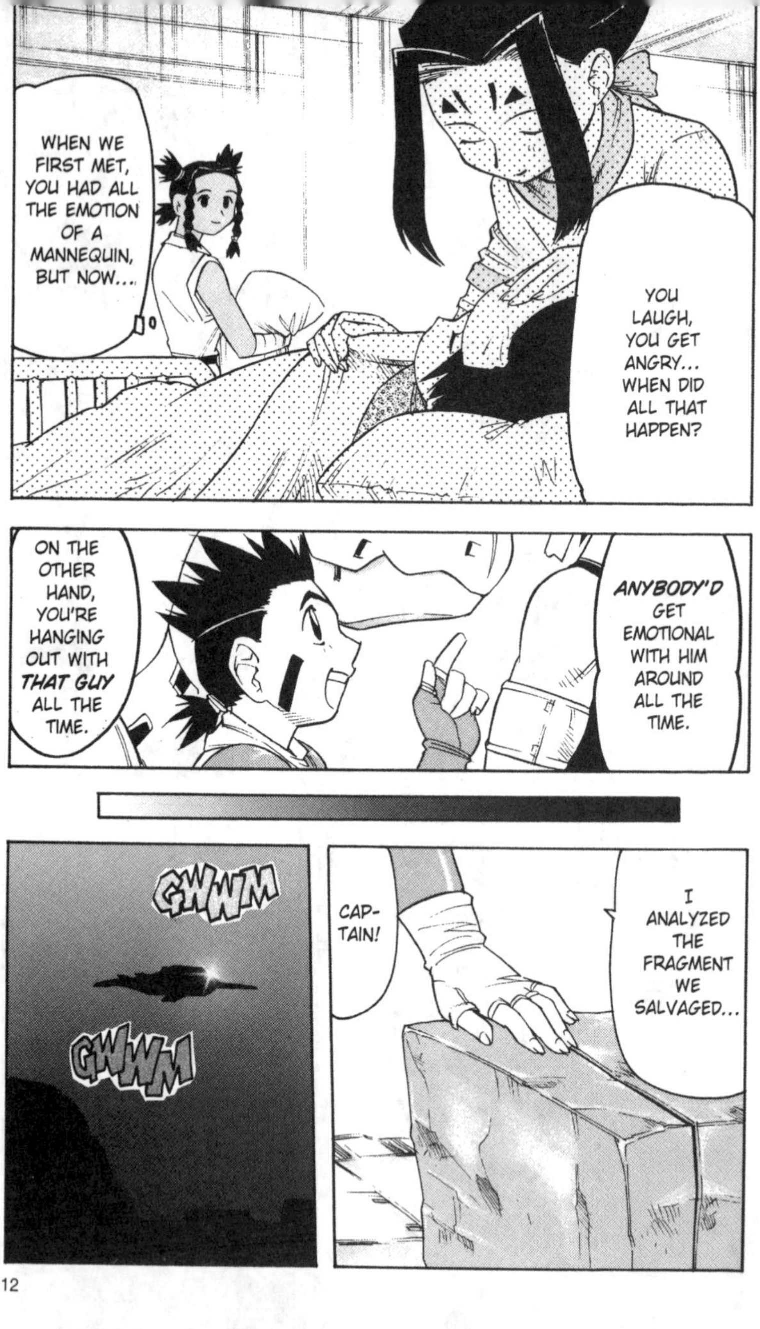
WHEN WE FIRST MET, YOU HAD ALL THE EMOTION OF A MANNEQUIN, BUT NOW...
YOU LAUGH, YOU GET ANGRY... WHEN DID ALL THAT HAPPEN?
ON THE OTHER HAND, YOU'RE HANGING OUT WITH *THAT GUY* ALL THE TIME.
ANYBODY'D GET EMOTIONAL WITH HIM AROUND ALL THE TIME.
GWWM
GWWM
CAP-TAIN!
I ANALYZED THE FRAGMENT WE SALVAGED...

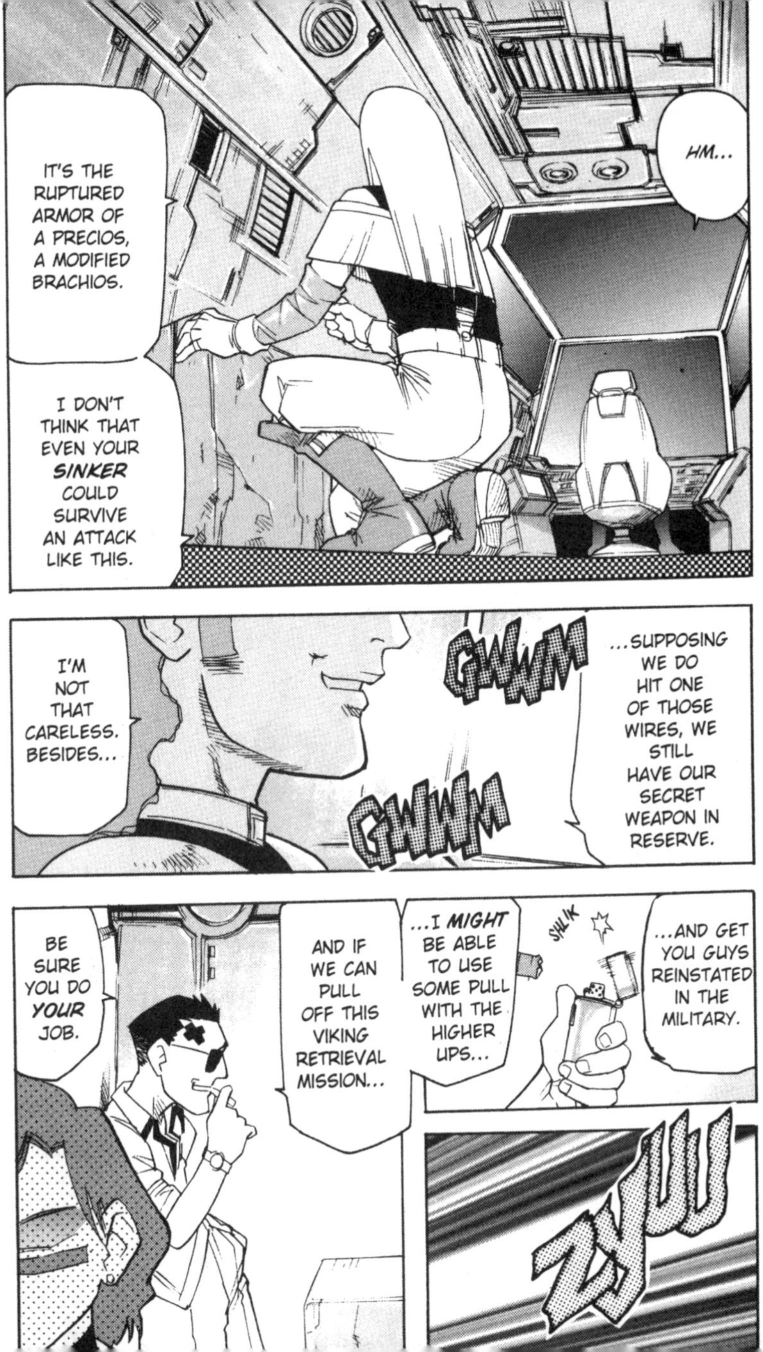
IT'S THE RUPTURED ARMOR OF A PRECIOS, A MODIFIED BRACHIOS.
I DON'T THINK THAT EVEN YOUR ***SINKER*** COULD SURVIVE AN ATTACK LIKE THIS.
HM...
I'M NOT THAT CARELESS. BESIDES...
GWWM
GWWM
...SUPPOSING WE DO HIT ONE OF THOSE WIRES, WE STILL HAVE OUR SECRET WEAPON IN RESERVE.
BE SURE YOU DO ***YOUR*** JOB.
AND IF WE CAN PULL OFF THIS VIKING RETRIEVAL MISSION...
...I ***MIGHT*** BE ABLE TO USE SOME PULL WITH THE HIGHER UPS...
SHLIK
...AND GET YOU GUYS REINSTATED IN THE MILITARY.
ZYUU

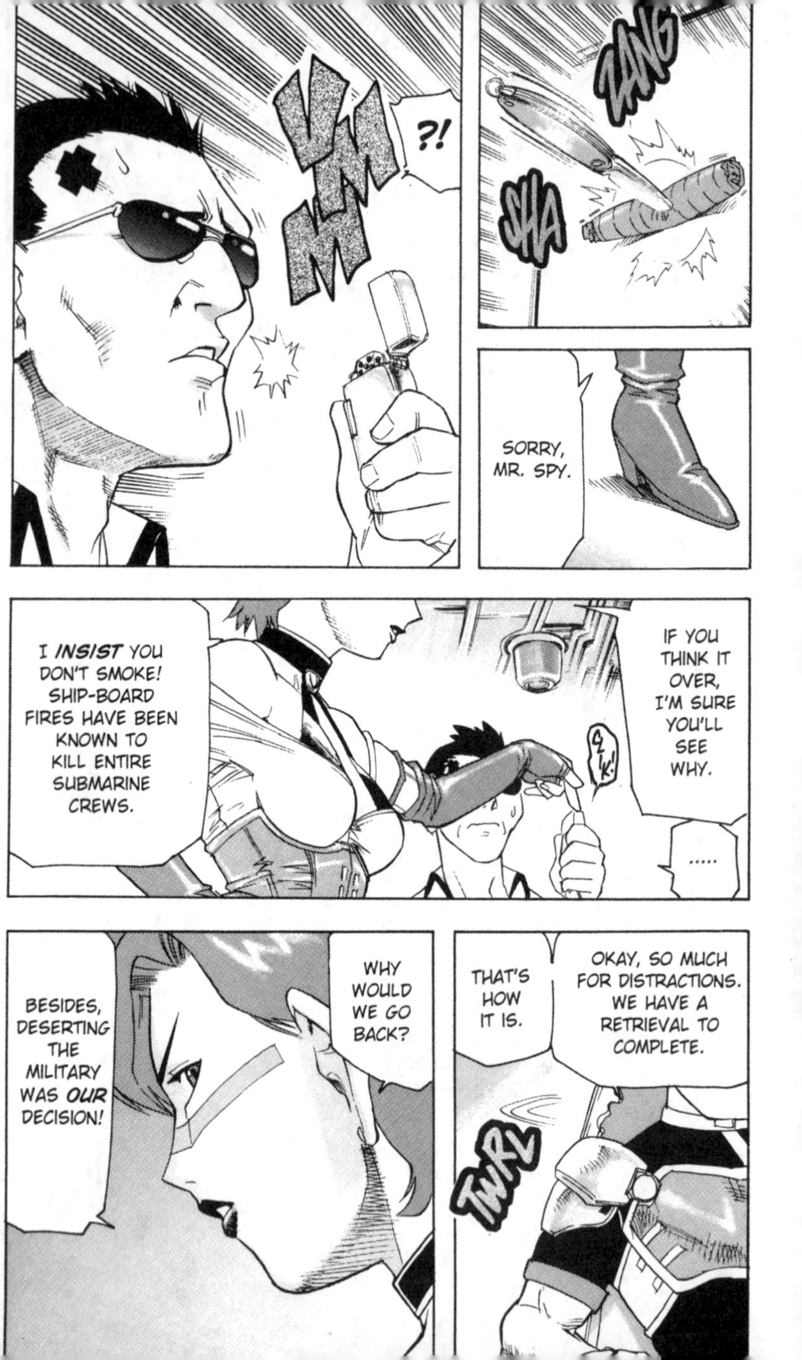

VMMM
?!
ZANG
SHA
SORRY, MR. SPY.
I *INSIST* YOU DON'T SMOKE! SHIP-BOARD FIRES HAVE BEEN KNOWN TO KILL ENTIRE SUBMARINE CREWS.
IF YOU THINK IT OVER, I'M SURE YOU'LL SEE WHY.
SLIK!
.....
BESIDES, DESERTING THE MILITARY WAS *OUR* DECISION!
WHY WOULD WE GO BACK?
THAT'S HOW IT IS.
OKAY, SO MUCH FOR DISTRACTIONS. WE HAVE A RETRIEVAL TO COMPLETE.
TWRL

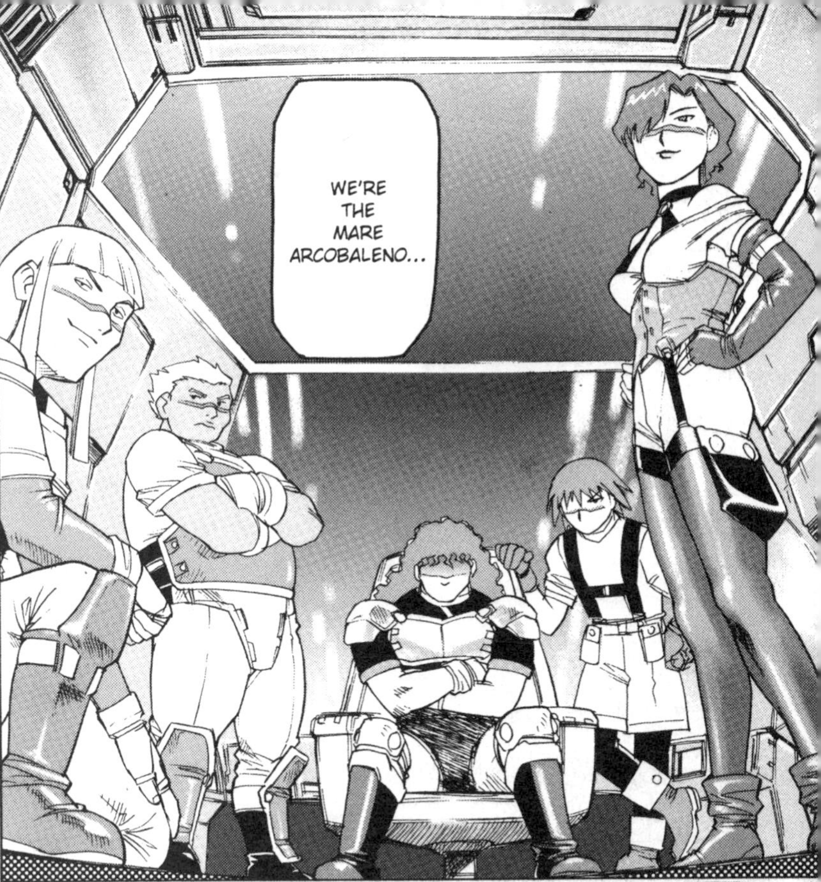
WE'RE THE MARE ARCOBALENO...
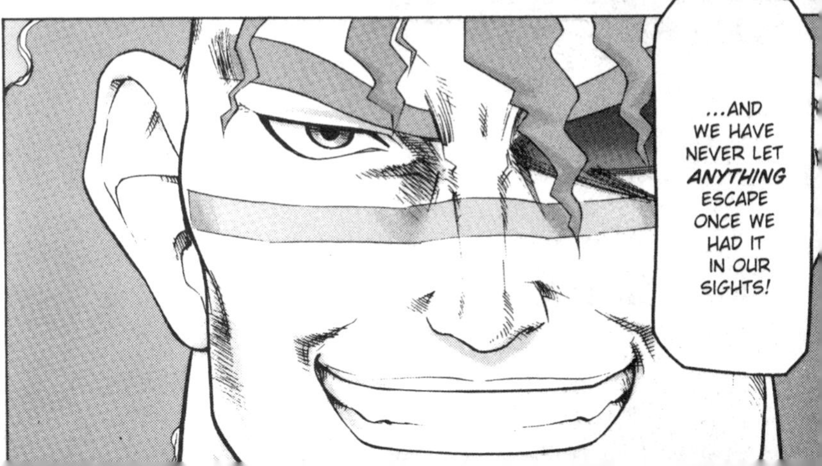
...AND WE HAVE NEVER LET ***ANYTHING*** ESCAPE ONCE WE HAD IT IN OUR SIGHTS!

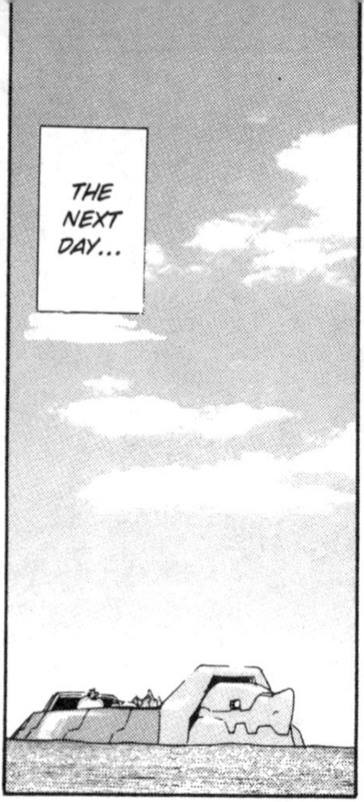
THE NEXT DAY...

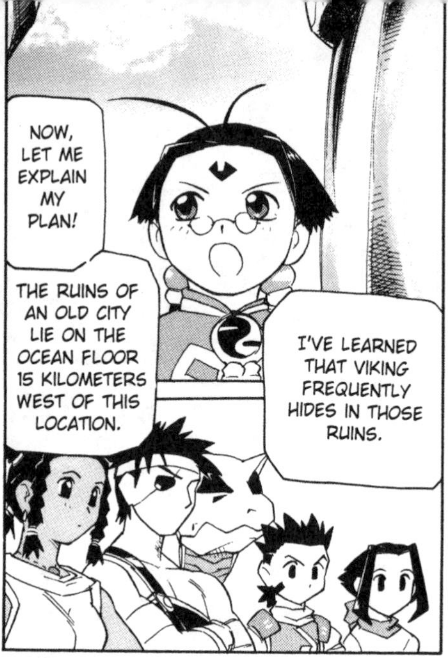
NOW, LET ME EXPLAIN MY PLAN!
THE RUINS OF AN OLD CITY LIE ON THE OCEAN FLOOR 15 KILOMETERS WEST OF THIS LOCATION.
I'VE LEARNED THAT VIKING FREQUENTLY HIDES IN THOSE RUINS.

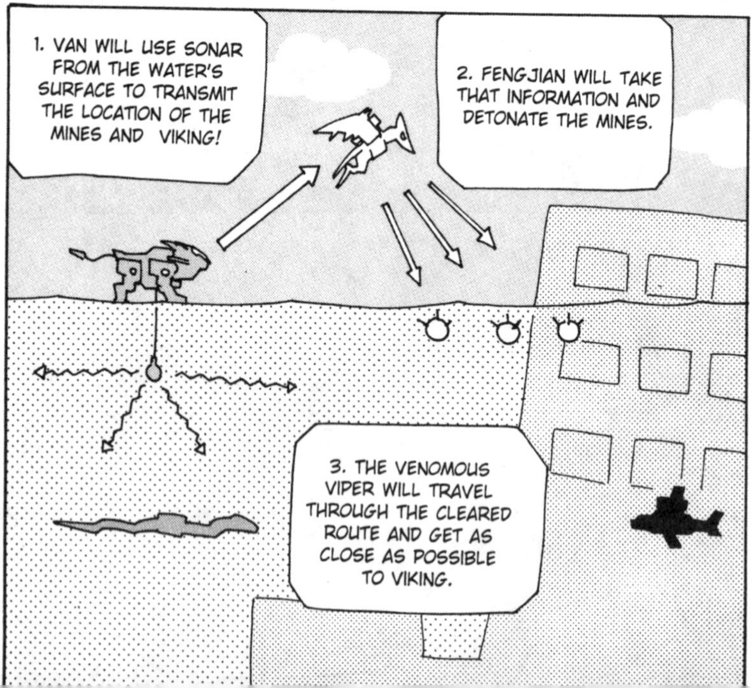
1. VAN WILL USE SONAR FROM THE WATER'S SURFACE TO TRANSMIT THE LOCATION OF THE MINES AND VIKING!
2. FENGJIAN WILL TAKE THAT INFORMATION AND DETONATE THE MINES.
3. THE VENOMOUS VIPER WILL TRAVEL THROUGH THE CLEARED ROUTE AND GET AS CLOSE AS POSSIBLE TO VIKING.

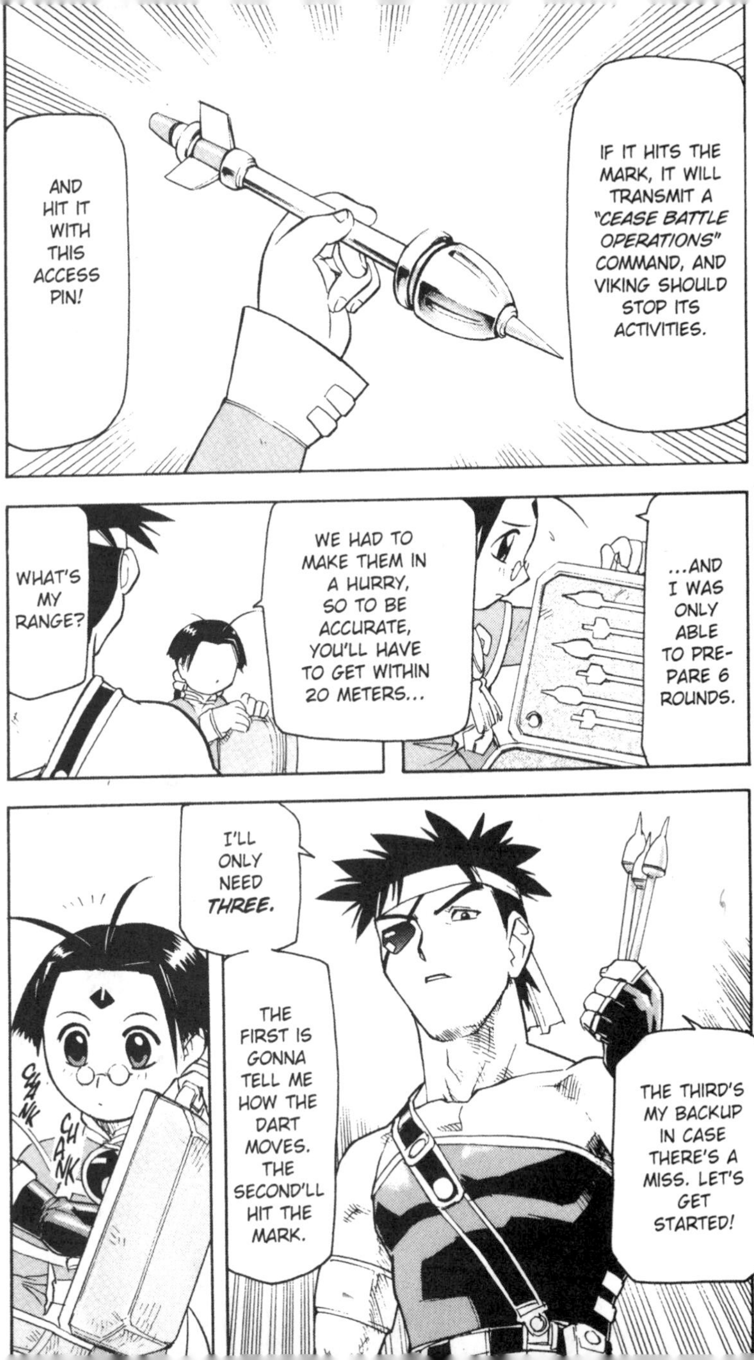
AND HIT IT WITH THIS ACCESS PIN!
IF IT HITS THE MARK, IT WILL TRANSMIT A "CEASE BATTLE OPERATIONS" COMMAND, AND VIKING SHOULD STOP ITS ACTIVITIES.
WHAT'S MY RANGE?
WE HAD TO MAKE THEM IN A HURRY, SO TO BE ACCURATE, YOU'LL HAVE TO GET WITHIN 20 METERS...
...AND I WAS ONLY ABLE TO PRE-PARE 6 ROUNDS.
I'LL ONLY NEED THREE.
CHANK
CHANK
THE FIRST IS GONNA TELL ME HOW THE DART MOVES. THE SECOND'LL HIT THE MARK.
THE THIRD'S MY BACKUP IN CASE THERE'S A MISS. LET'S GET STARTED!

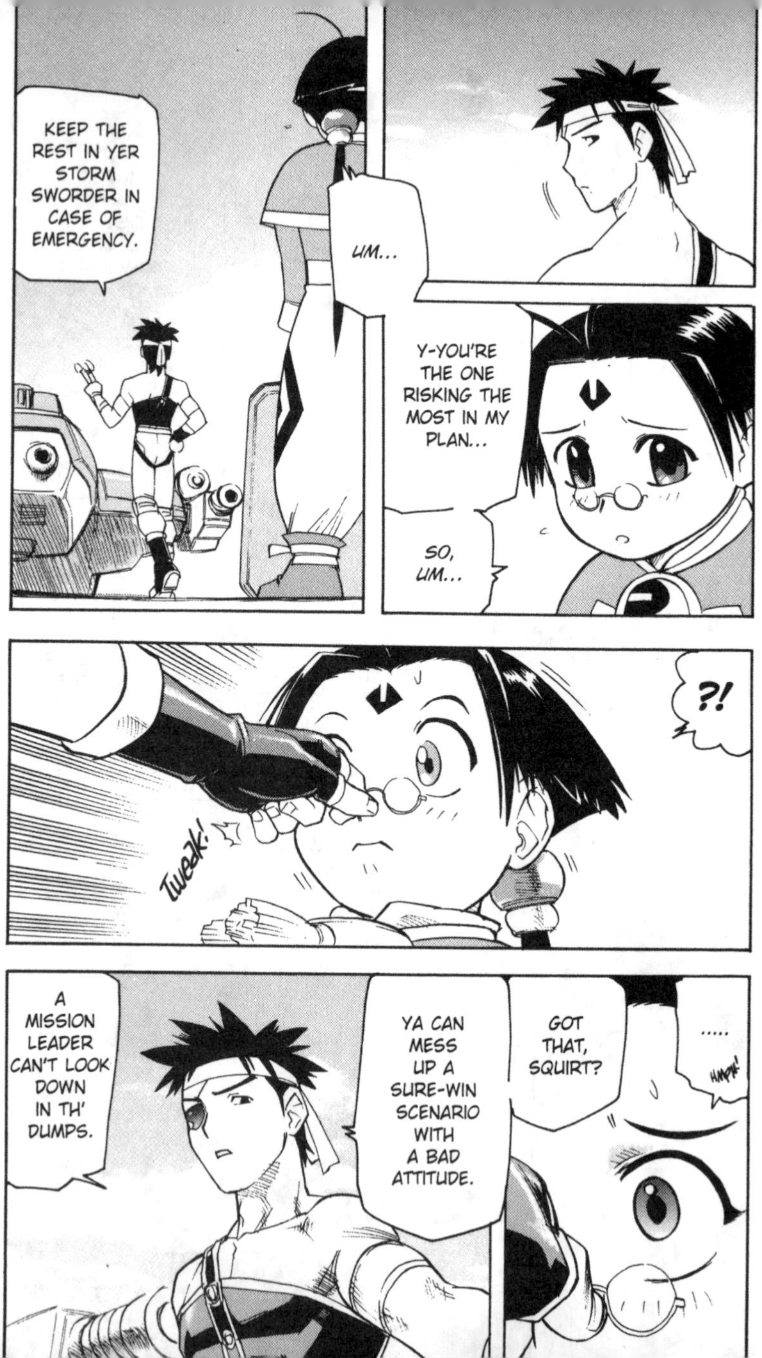
KEEP THE REST IN YER STORM SWORDER IN CASE OF EMERGENCY.
UM...
Y-YOU'RE THE ONE RISKING THE MOST IN MY PLAN...
SO, UM...
?!
TWEAK!
A MISSION LEADER CAN'T LOOK DOWN IN TH' DUMPS.
YA CAN MESS UP A SURE-WIN SCENARIO WITH A BAD ATTITUDE.
GOT THAT, SQUIRT?
.....
HMPH!

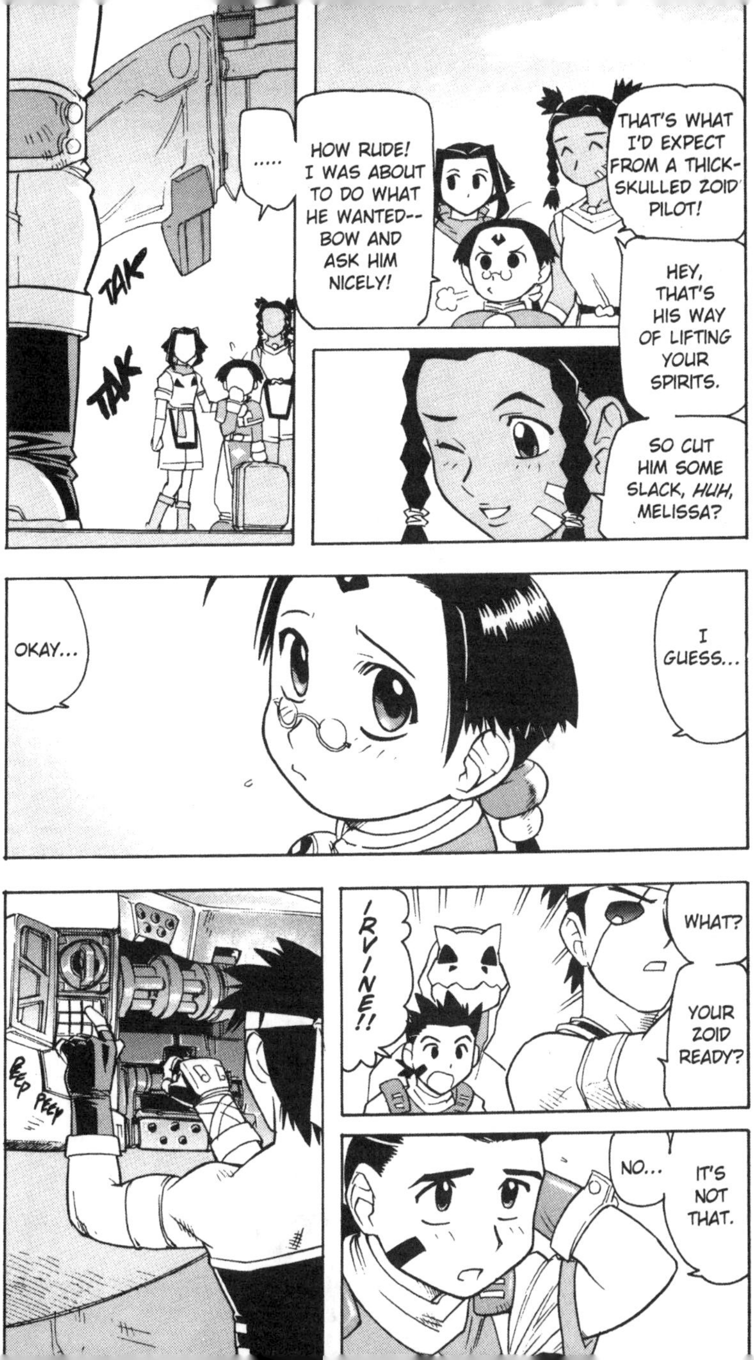

TAK
TAK
.....
HOW RUDE! I WAS ABOUT TO DO WHAT HE WANTED-- BOW AND ASK HIM NICELY!
THAT'S WHAT I'D EXPECT FROM A THICK-SKULLED ZOID PILOT!
HEY, THAT'S HIS WAY OF LIFTING YOUR SPIRITS.
SO CUT HIM SOME SLACK, *HUH*, MELISSA?
OKAY...
I GUESS...
BEEP BEEP
IRVINE!!
WHAT?
YOUR ZOID READY?
NO...
IT'S NOT THAT.

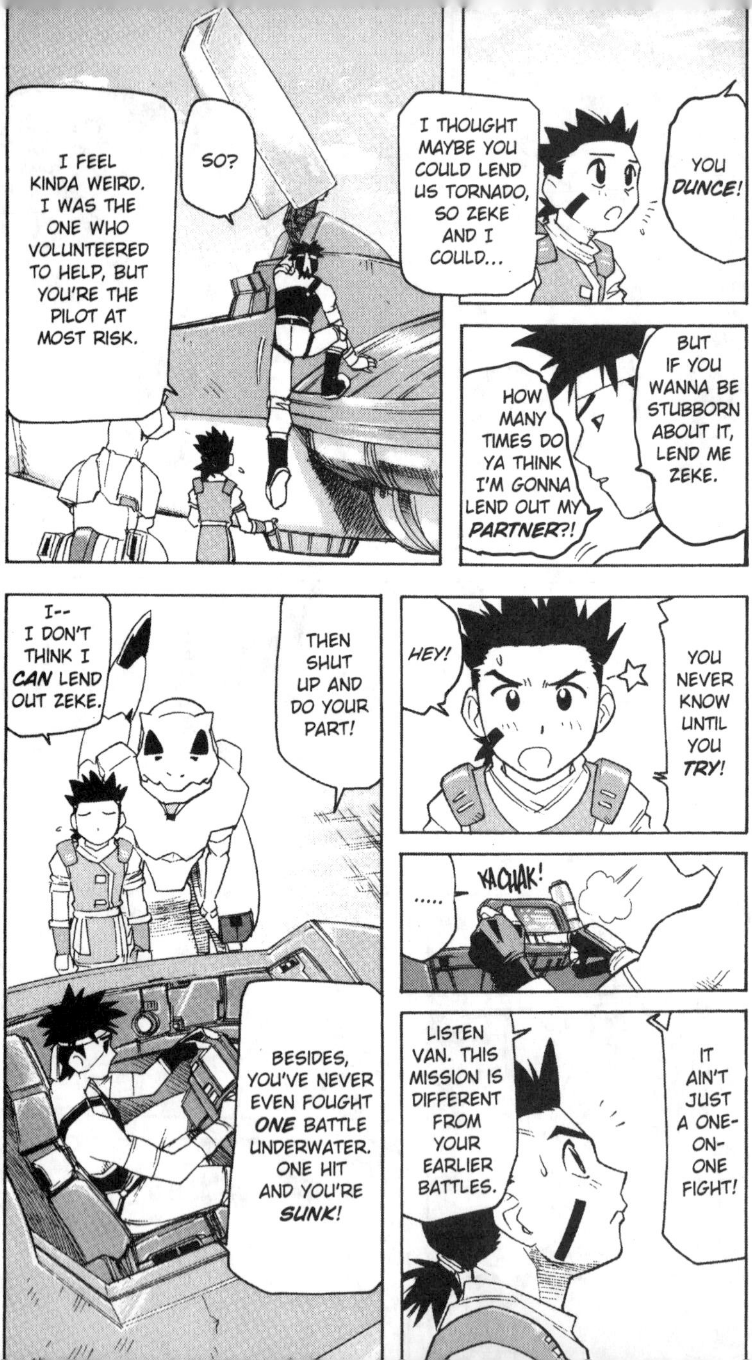
I FEEL KINDA WEIRD. I WAS THE ONE WHO VOLUNTEERED TO HELP, BUT YOU'RE THE PILOT AT MOST RISK.
SO?
I THOUGHT MAYBE YOU COULD LEND US TORNADO, SO ZEKE AND I COULD...
YOU DUNCE!
HOW MANY TIMES DO YA THINK I'M GONNA LEND OUT MY PARTNER?!
BUT IF YOU WANNA BE STUBBORN ABOUT IT, LEND ME ZEKE.
I-- I DON'T THINK I CAN LEND OUT ZEKE.
THEN SHUT UP AND DO YOUR PART!
HEY!
YOU NEVER KNOW UNTIL YOU TRY!
.....
KACHAK!
BESIDES, YOU'VE NEVER EVEN FOUGHT ONE BATTLE UNDERWATER. ONE HIT AND YOU'RE SUNK!
LISTEN VAN. THIS MISSION IS DIFFERENT FROM YOUR EARLIER BATTLES.
IT AIN'T JUST A ONE-ON-ONE FIGHT!

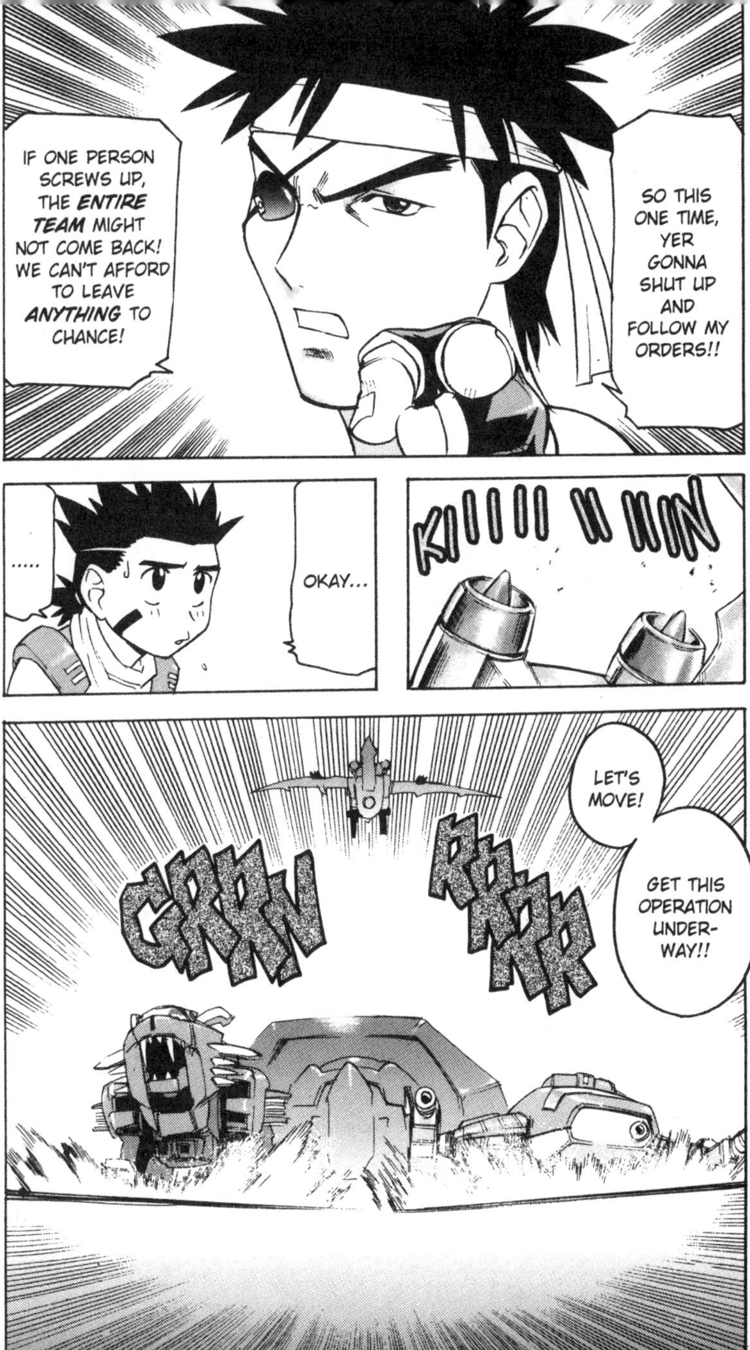
IF ONE PERSON SCREWS UP, THE *ENTIRE TEAM* MIGHT NOT COME BACK! WE CAN'T AFFORD TO LEAVE *ANYTHING* TO CHANCE!
SO THIS ONE TIME, YER GONNA SHUT UP AND FOLLOW MY ORDERS!!
.....
OKAY...
KIIIII II IIIN
LET'S MOVE!
GET THIS OPERATION UNDER-WAY!!
GRRN
RRRRR

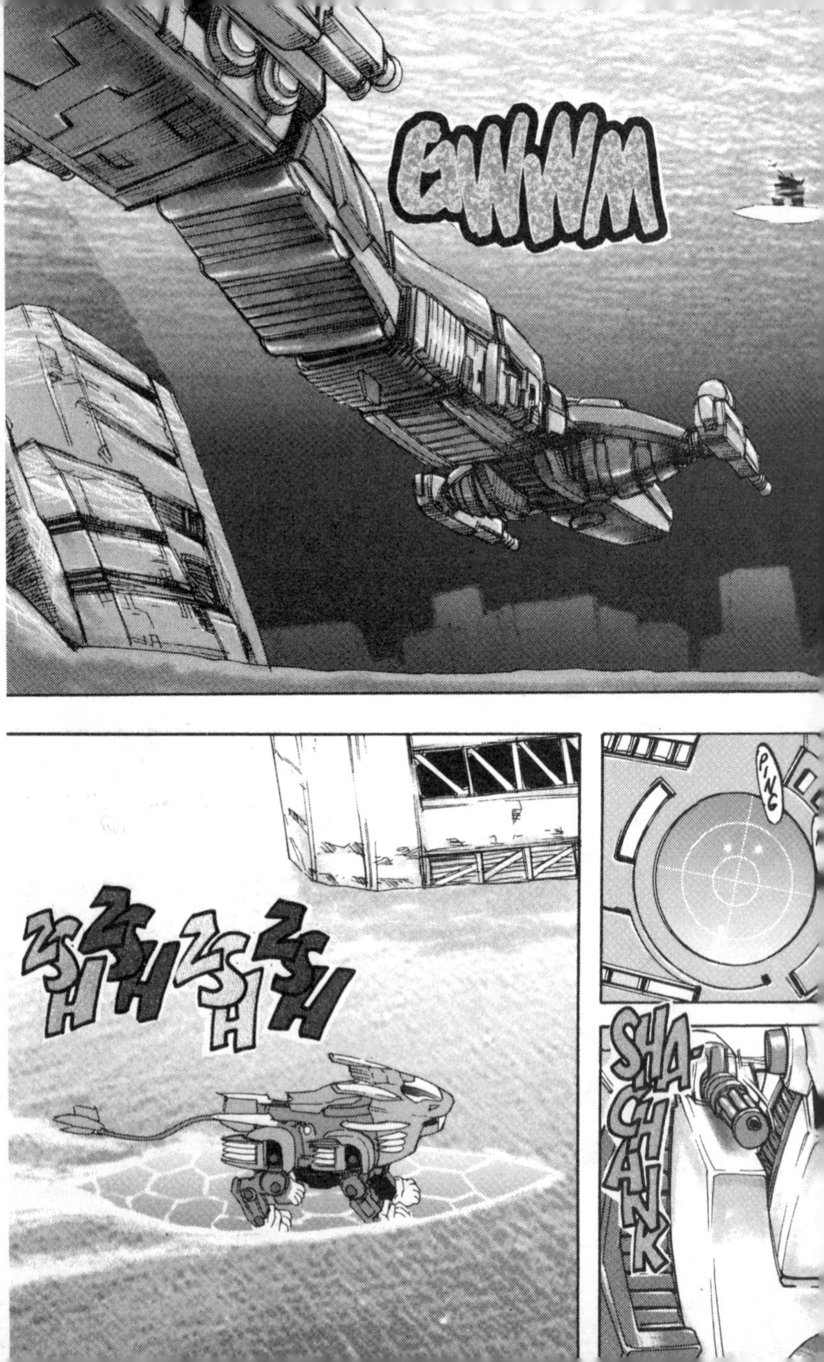
GWWM
PING
SHACHACHANK
ZSH ZSH ZSH ZSH

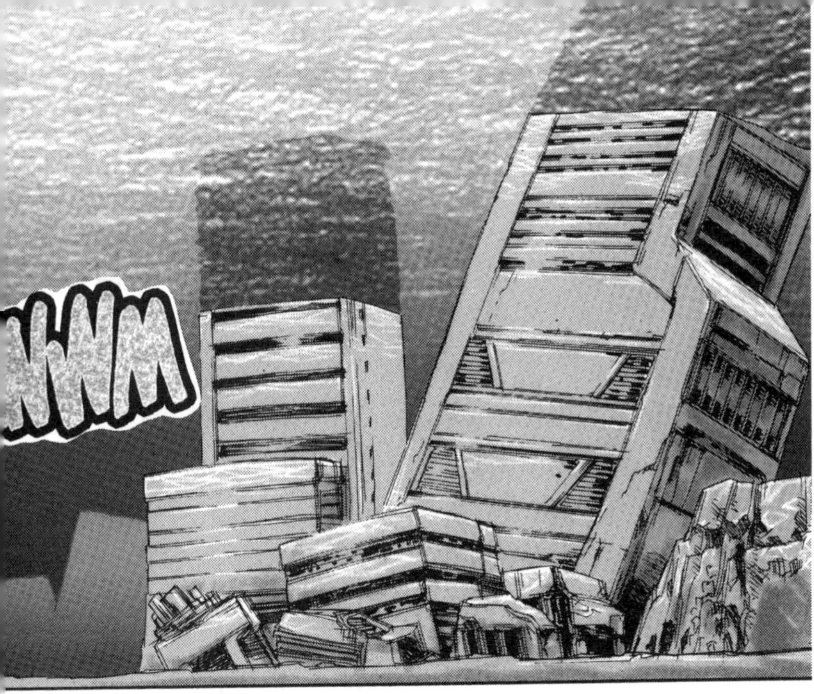
NNM
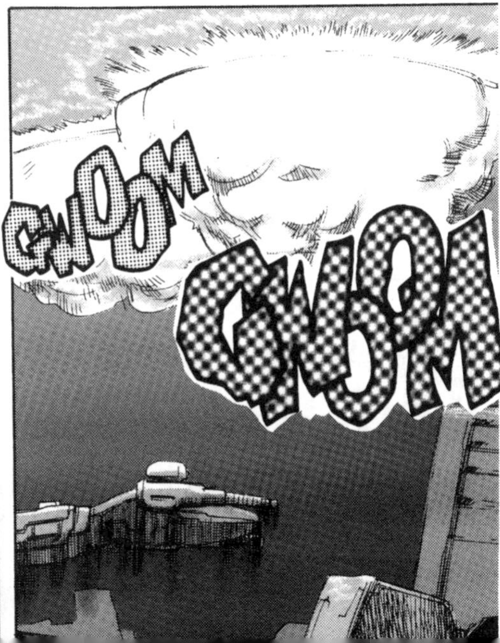
GWOOM
GWOOM
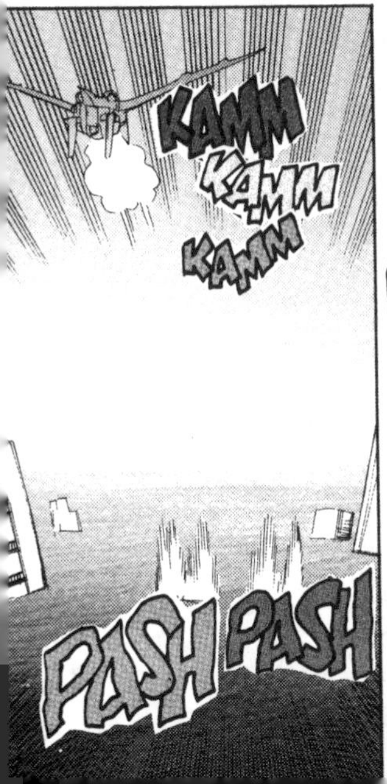
KAMM
KAMM
KAMM
PASH
PASH

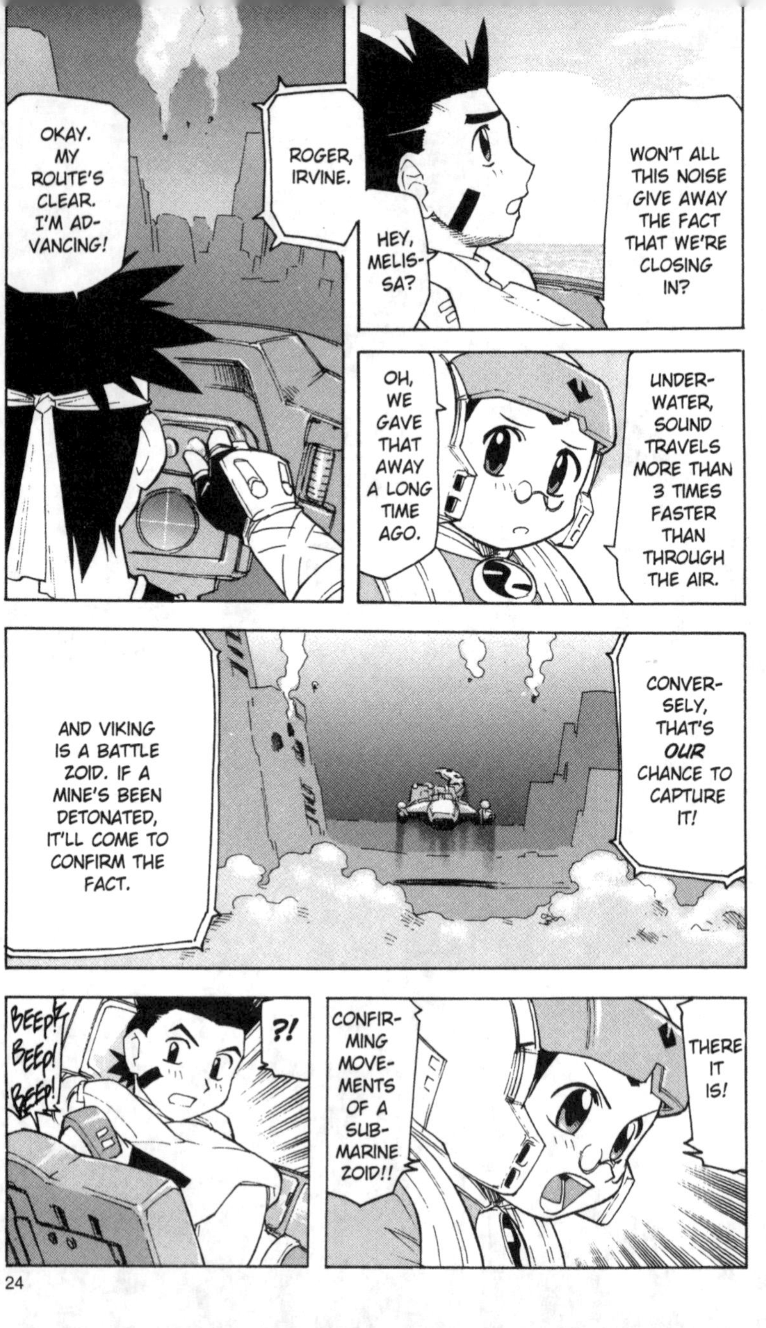
OKAY. MY ROUTE'S CLEAR. I'M AD-VANCING!
ROGER, IRVINE.
WON'T ALL THIS NOISE GIVE AWAY THE FACT THAT WE'RE CLOSING IN?
HEY, MELIS-SA?
OH, WE GAVE THAT AWAY A LONG TIME AGO.
UNDER-WATER, SOUND TRAVELS MORE THAN 3 TIMES FASTER THAN THROUGH THE AIR.
AND VIKING IS A BATTLE ZOID. IF A MINE'S BEEN DETONATED, IT'LL COME TO CONFIRM THE FACT.
CONVER-SELY, THAT'S *OUR* CHANCE TO CAPTURE IT!
BEEP BEEP! BEEP!
?!
CONFIR-MING MOVE-MENTS OF A SUB-MARINE ZOID!!
THERE IT IS!

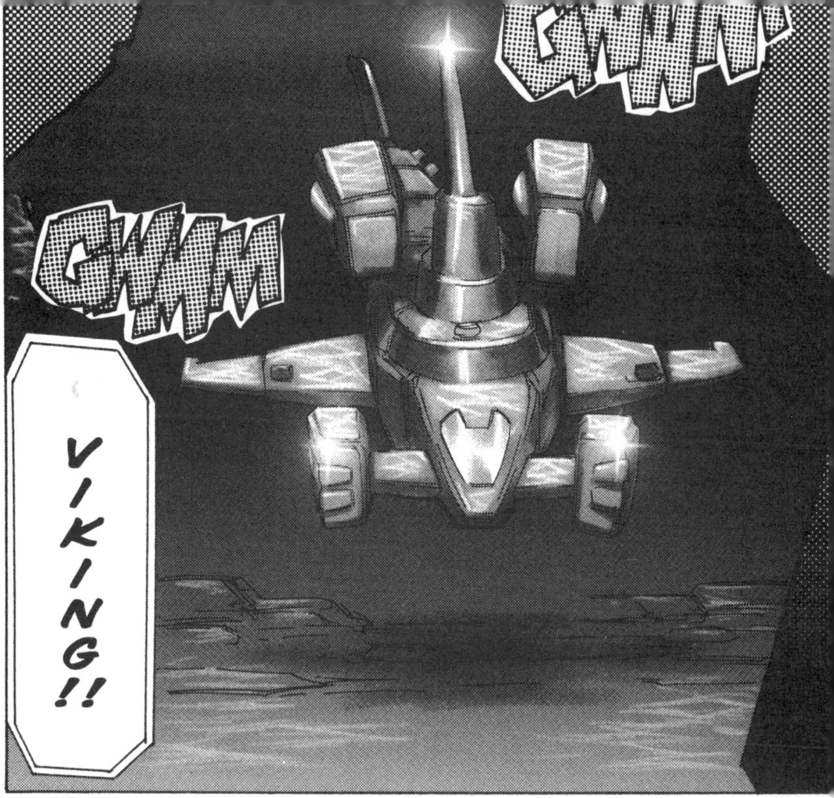
GWWM
VIKING!!
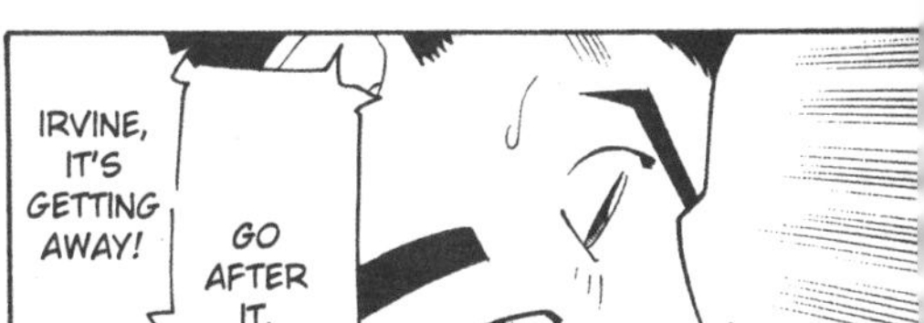
IRVINE, IT'S GETTING AWAY!
GO AFTER IT, OR--
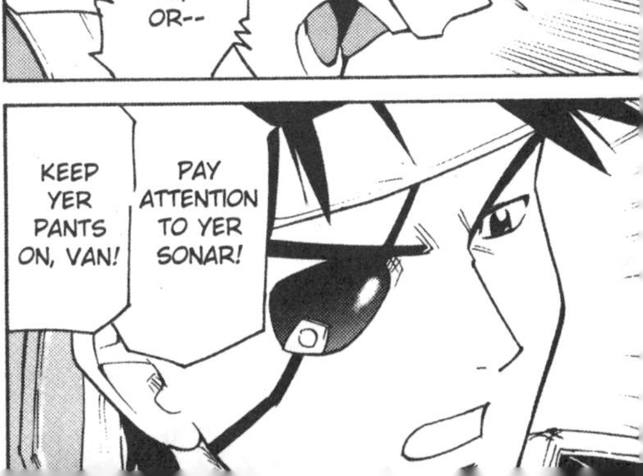
PAY ATTENTION TO YER SONAR!
KEEP YER PANTS ON, VAN!
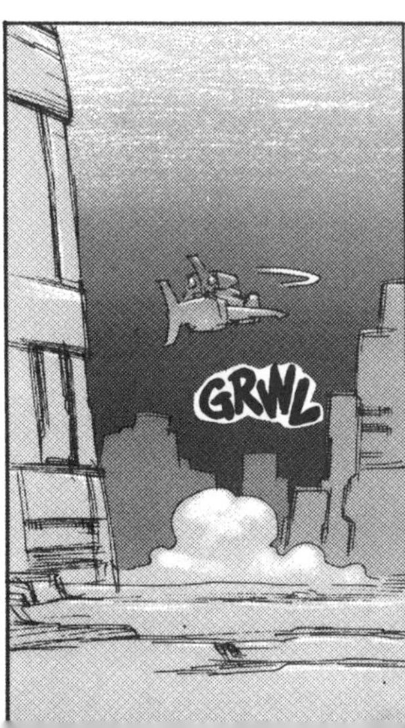
GRWL

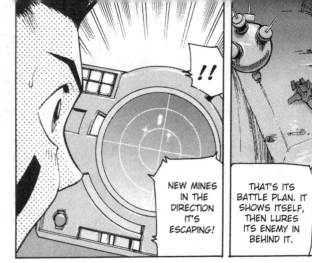

NEW MINES IN THE DIRECTION IT'S ESCAPING!

THAT'S ITS BATTLE PLAN. IT SHOWS ITSELF, THEN LURES ITS ENEMY IN BEHIND IT.

ANYBODY GOES CHASIN' BLINDLY AFTER IT, AND *KABOOM!*

GOOD THING THE SQUIRT MADE THIS MINE-SENSING SONAR.

ALL WE GOTTA DO IS DETONATE 'EM ALL, AND WE'LL CATCH UP EVENTUALLY!

LISTEN UP! THIS IS A HUNT! SO AGILITY AND ACCURACY DON'T MATTER MUCH HERE!

WHAT WE'RE DOIN' IS SEEIN' HOW IT ACTS AND USIN' THAT TO OUR ADVANTAGE!

NOW LET'S GET BUSY PINPOINTIN' THOSE MINES!

O-- OKAY!

HM...

MAYBE HE *DOES* UNDER-STAND...

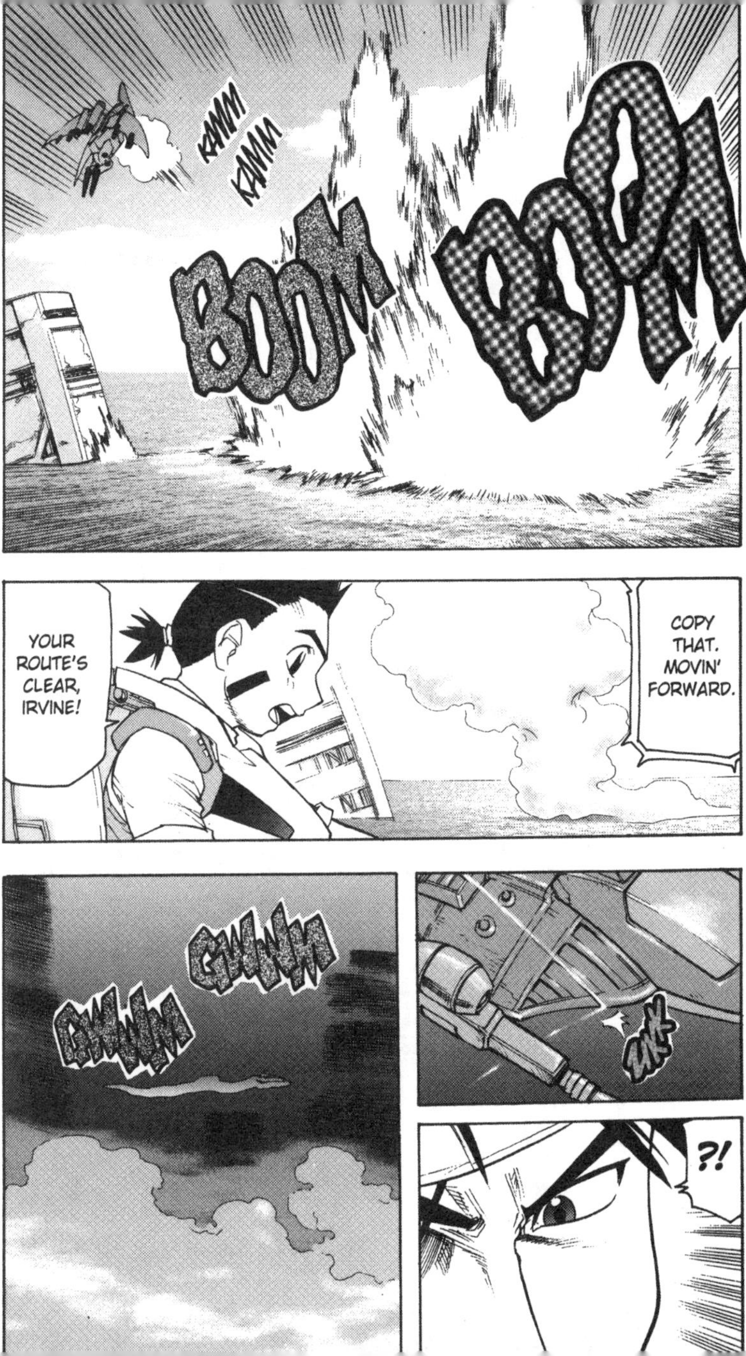
KAMM
KAMM
BOOM
BOOM
YOUR ROUTE'S CLEAR, IRVINE!
COPY THAT. MOVIN' FORWARD.
GWWM
GWWM
ZUK
?!

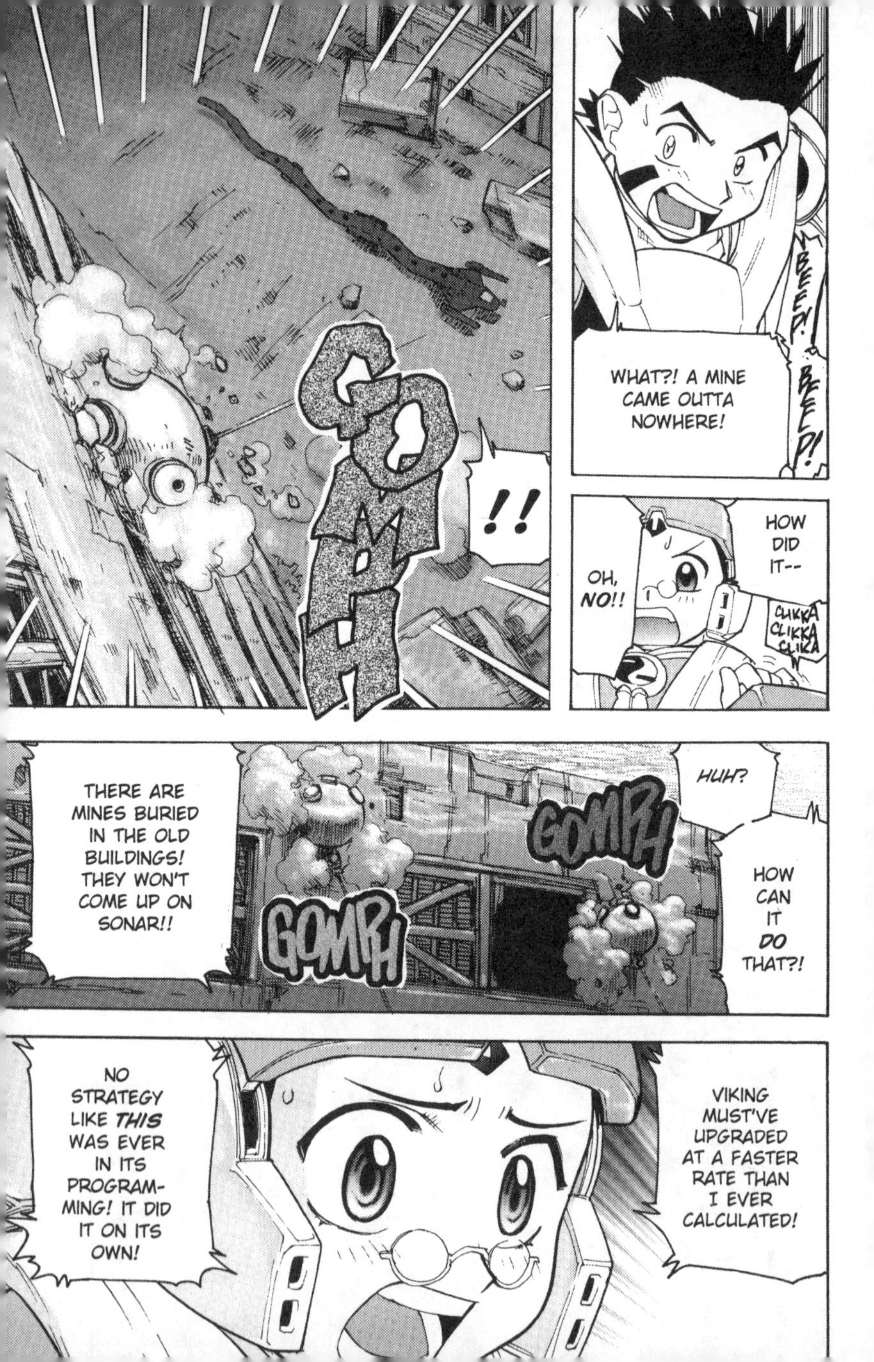
WHAT?! A MINE CAME OUTTA NOWHERE!
BEEP! BEEP!
HOW DID IT--
OH, NO!!
CLIKKA CLIKKA CLIKKA
!!
GOMPH
HUH?
HOW CAN IT DO THAT?!
GOMPH
GOMPH
THERE ARE MINES BURIED IN THE OLD BUILDINGS! THEY WON'T COME UP ON SONAR!!
VIKING MUST'VE UPGRADED AT A FASTER RATE THAN I EVER CALCULATED!
NO STRATEGY LIKE THIS WAS EVER IN ITS PROGRAMMING! IT DID IT ON ITS OWN!

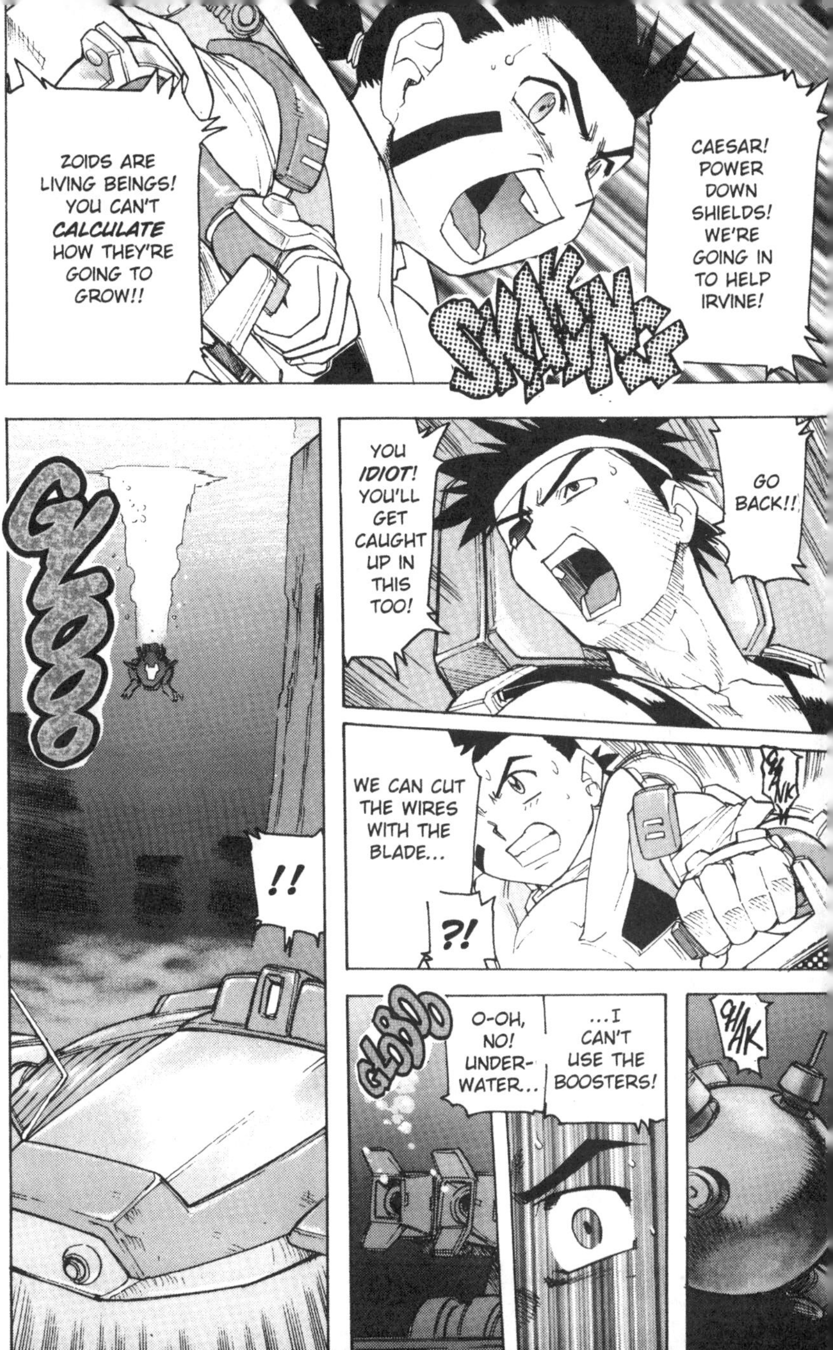
CAESAR! POWER DOWN SHIELDS! WE'RE GOING IN TO HELP IRVINE!
ZOIDS ARE LIVING BEINGS! YOU CAN'T *CALCULATE* HOW THEY'RE GOING TO GROW!!
GO BACK!!
YOU *IDIOT*! YOU'LL GET CAUGHT UP IN THIS TOO!
WE CAN CUT THE WIRES WITH THE BLADE...
?!
!!
O-OH, NO! UNDER-WATER...
...I CAN'T USE THE BOOSTERS!

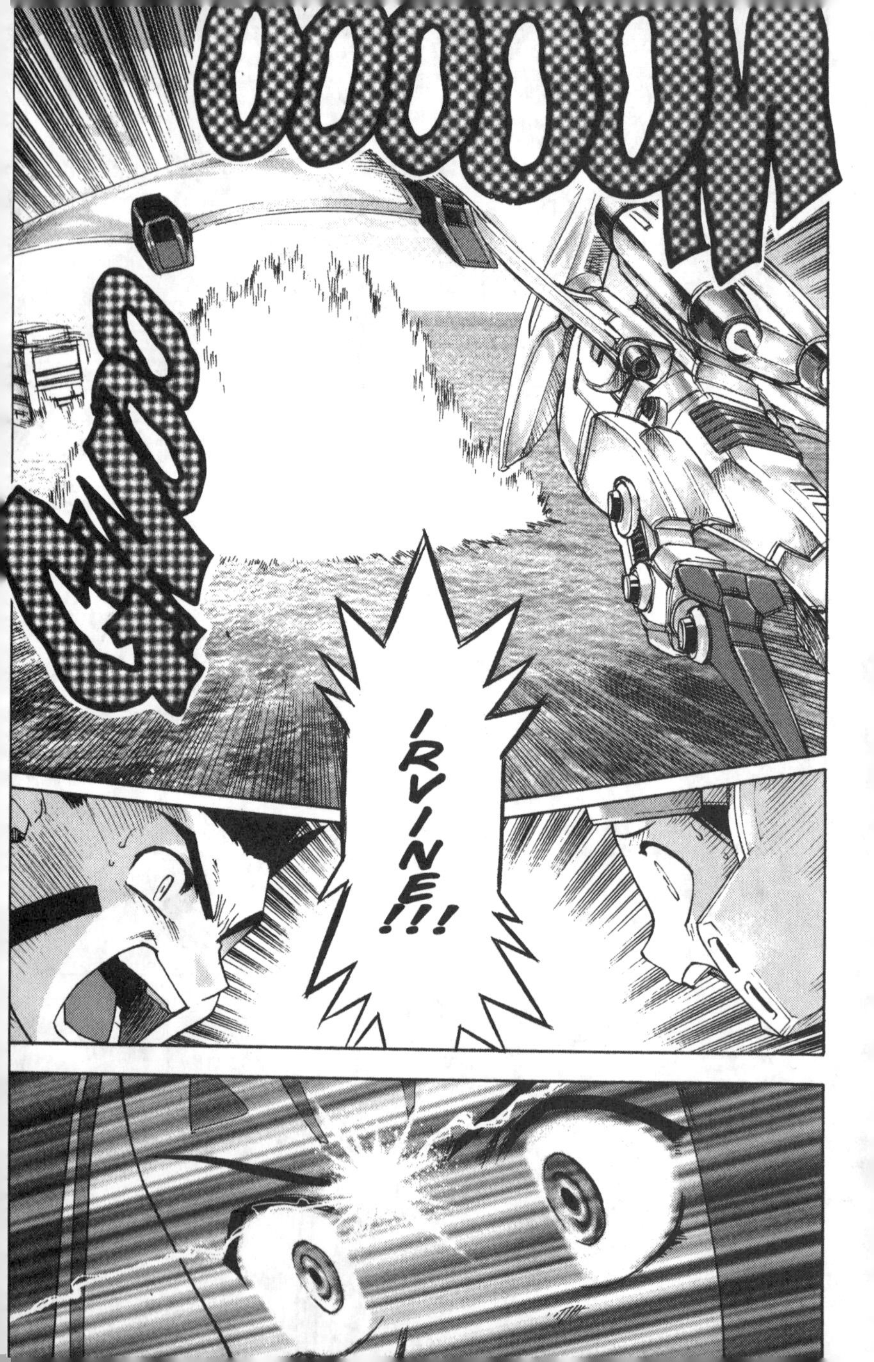
IRVINE!!!

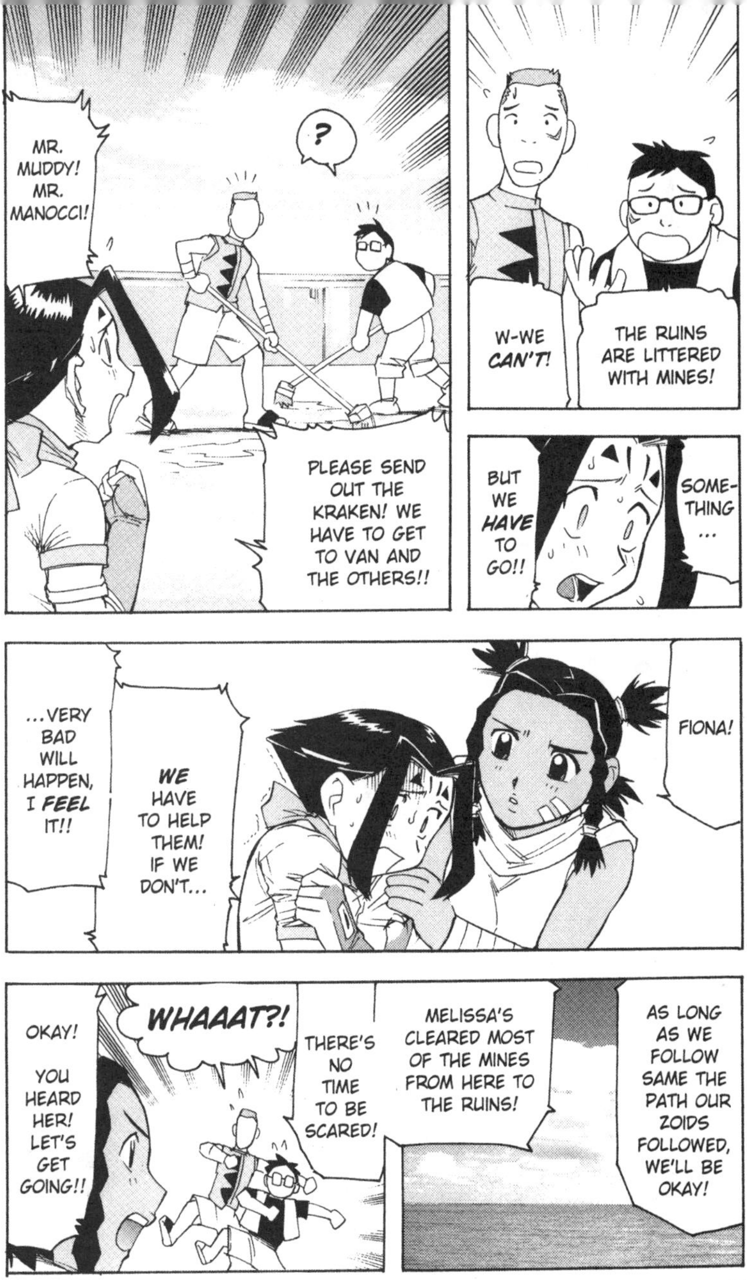
MR. MUDDY! MR. MANOCCI!
?
PLEASE SEND OUT THE KRAKEN! WE HAVE TO GET TO VAN AND THE OTHERS!!
W-WE CAN'T!
THE RUINS ARE LITTERED WITH MINES!
BUT WE HAVE TO GO!!
SOME-THING...
...VERY BAD WILL HAPPEN, I FEEL IT!!
WE HAVE TO HELP THEM! IF WE DON'T...
FIONA!
OKAY! YOU HEARD HER! LET'S GET GOING!!
WHAAAT?!
THERE'S NO TIME TO BE SCARED!
MELISSA'S CLEARED MOST OF THE MINES FROM HERE TO THE RUINS!
AS LONG AS WE FOLLOW SAME THE PATH OUR ZOIDS FOLLOWED, WE'LL BE OKAY!

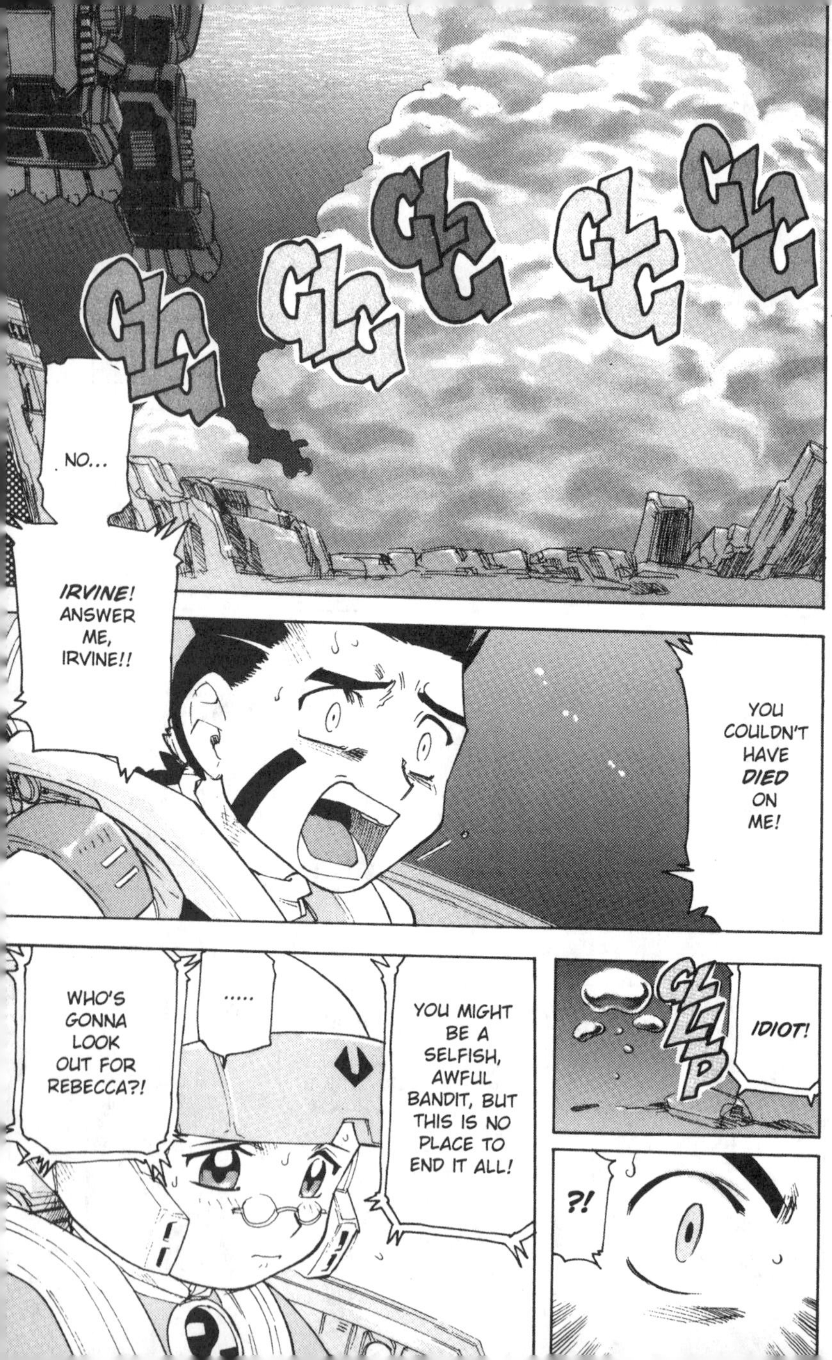
GLG GLG GLG GLG GLG
NO...
IRVINE! ANSWER ME, IRVINE!!
YOU COULDN'T HAVE *DIED* ON ME!
IDIOT!
GLLLP
YOU MIGHT BE A SELFISH, AWFUL BANDIT, BUT THIS IS NO PLACE TO END IT ALL!
.....
WHO'S GONNA LOOK OUT FOR REBECCA?!
?!

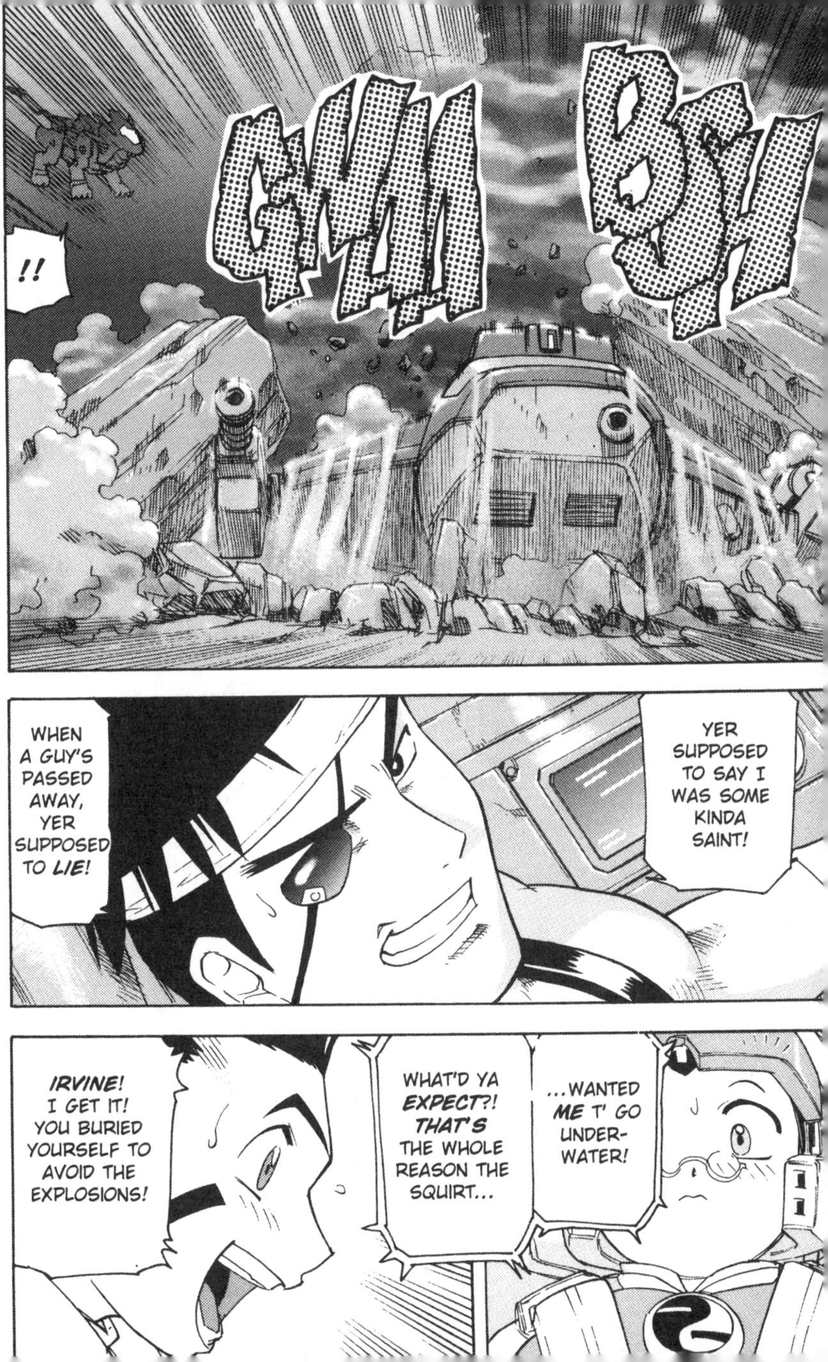
!!
WHEN A GUY'S PASSED AWAY, YER SUPPOSED TO *LIE*!
YER SUPPOSED TO SAY I WAS SOME KINDA SAINT!
IRVINE! I GET IT! YOU BURIED YOURSELF TO AVOID THE EXPLOSIONS!
WHAT'D YA *EXPECT*?! *THAT'S* THE WHOLE REASON THE SQUIRT...
...WANTED *ME* T' GO UNDER-WATER!

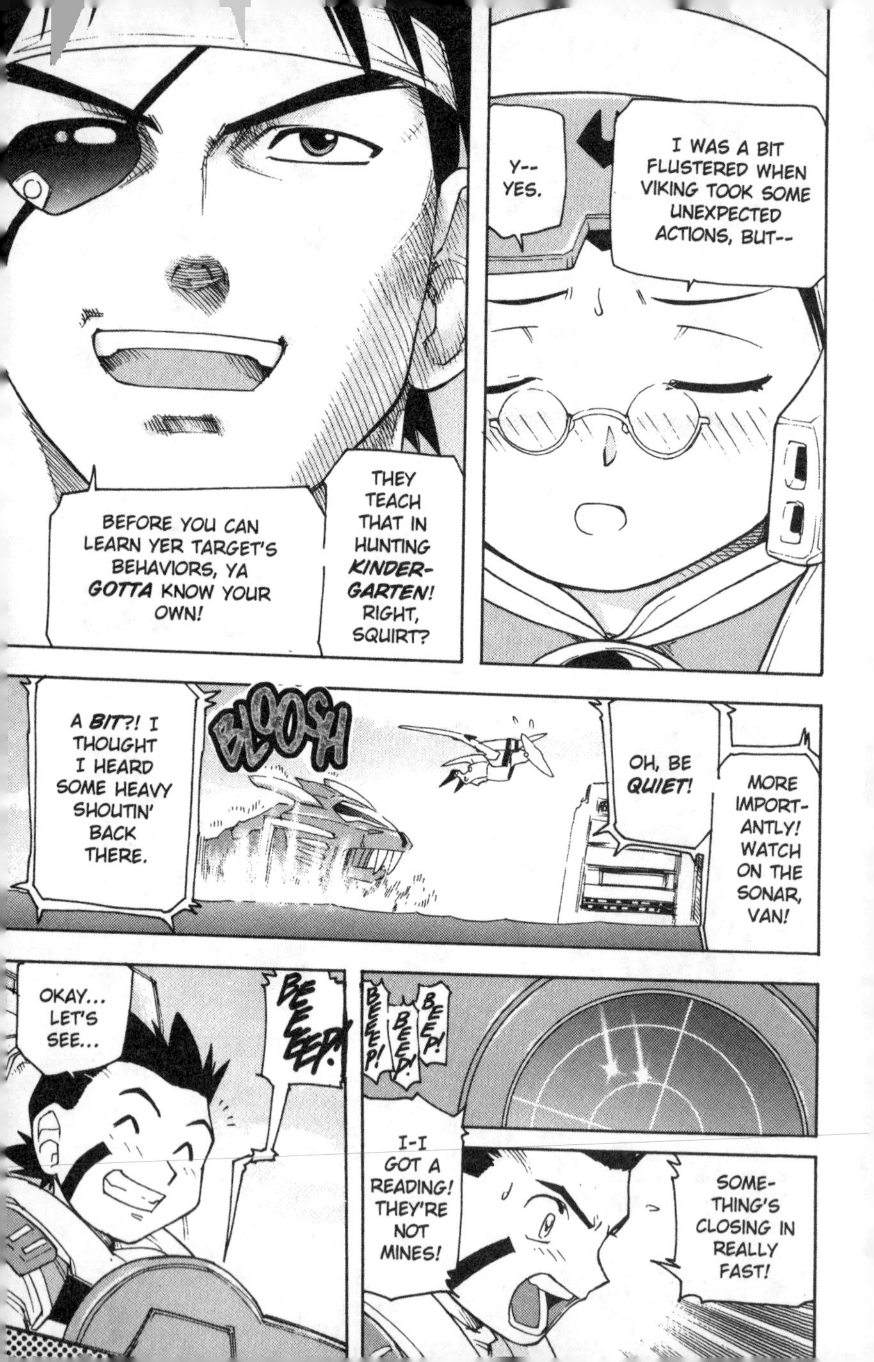

BEFORE YOU CAN LEARN YER TARGET'S BEHAVIORS, YA GOTTA KNOW YOUR OWN!
THEY TEACH THAT IN HUNTING KINDERGARTEN! RIGHT, SQUIRT?
Y-- YES.
I WAS A BIT FLUSTERED WHEN VIKING TOOK SOME UNEXPECTED ACTIONS, BUT--
A BIT?! I THOUGHT I HEARD SOME HEAVY SHOUTIN' BACK THERE.
BLOOSH
OH, BE QUIET!
MORE IMPORTANTLY! WATCH ON THE SONAR, VAN!
OKAY... LET'S SEE...
BEEEEEP!
BEEEP! BEEP! BEEP!
I-I GOT A READING! THEY'RE NOT MINES!
SOMETHING'S CLOSING IN REALLY FAST!

SYUUUUUU

GHSH!

KGRRR

SHORSH

IT'S BREAKING UP! GET OUT, IRVINE!!

KH!

GHKGHK!

THAT'S *IMPOSSIBLE!* VIKING ISN'T EQUIPPED WITH TORPEDOES!

WHO COULD POSSIBLY...?!

GM GM

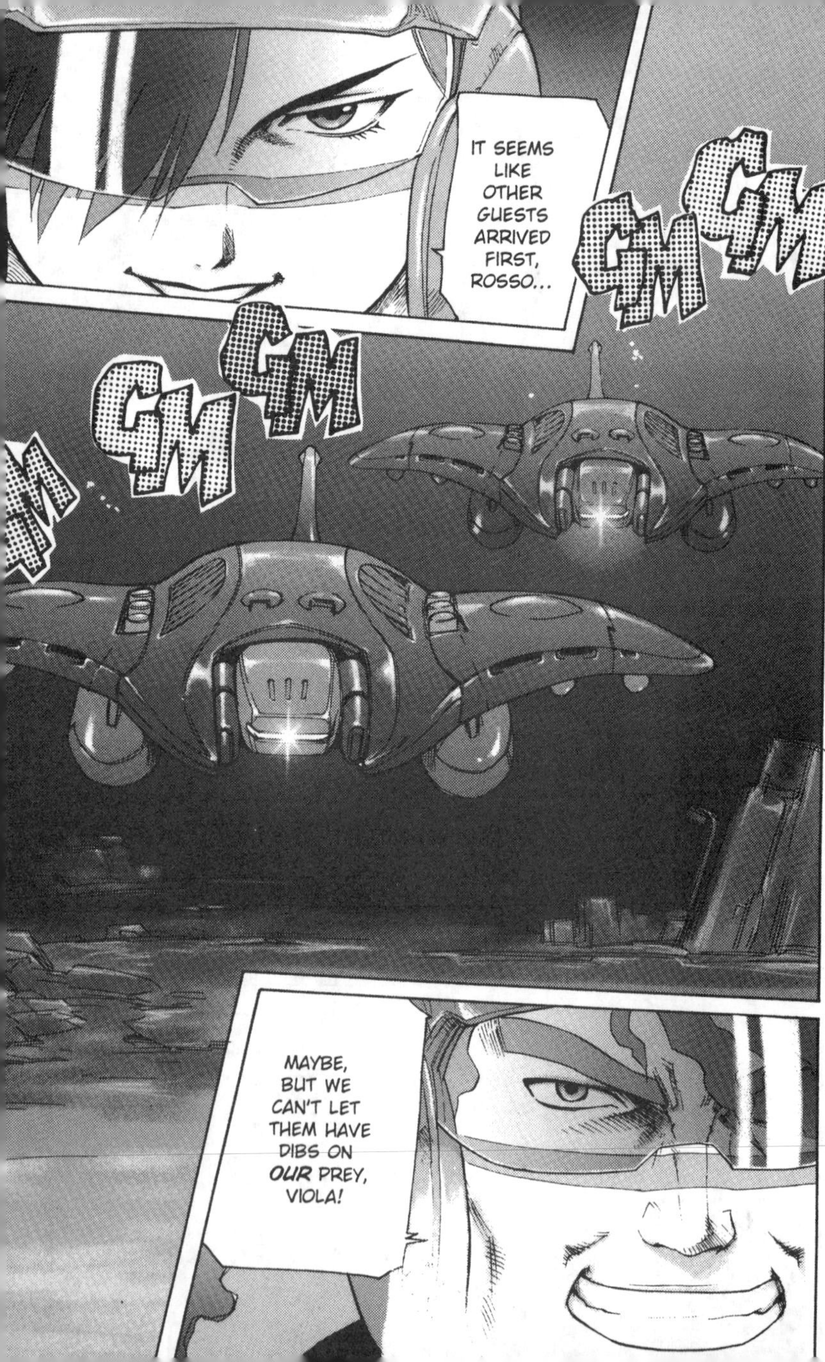
IT SEEMS LIKE OTHER GUESTS ARRIVED FIRST, ROSSO...
GM GM
GM
GM
MAYBE, BUT WE CAN'T LET THEM HAVE DIBS ON **OUR** PREY, VIOLA!

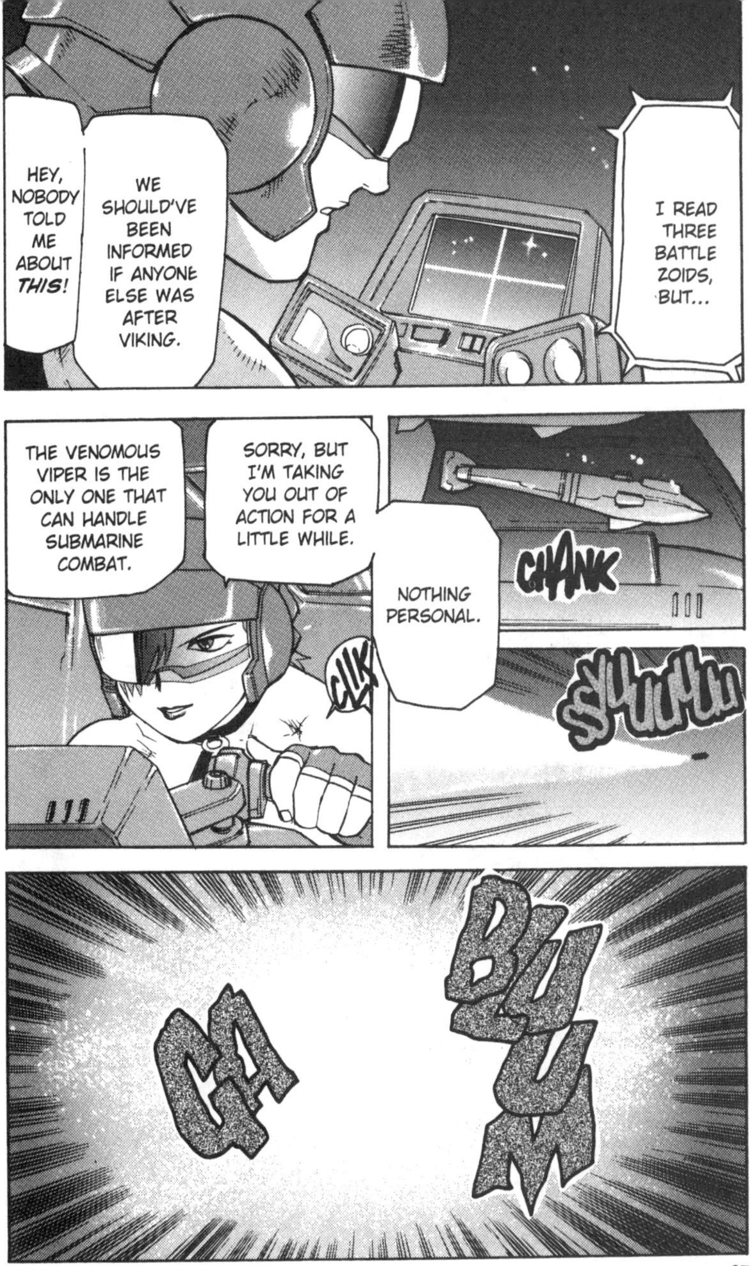
HEY, NOBODY TOLD ME ABOUT *THIS*!
WE SHOULD'VE BEEN INFORMED IF ANYONE ELSE WAS AFTER VIKING.
I READ THREE BATTLE ZOIDS, BUT...
THE VENOMOUS VIPER IS THE ONLY ONE THAT CAN HANDLE SUBMARINE COMBAT.
SORRY, BUT I'M TAKING YOU OUT OF ACTION FOR A LITTLE WHILE.
NOTHING PERSONAL.
CLIK
CHANK
SHUUUUU
GA
BUUM

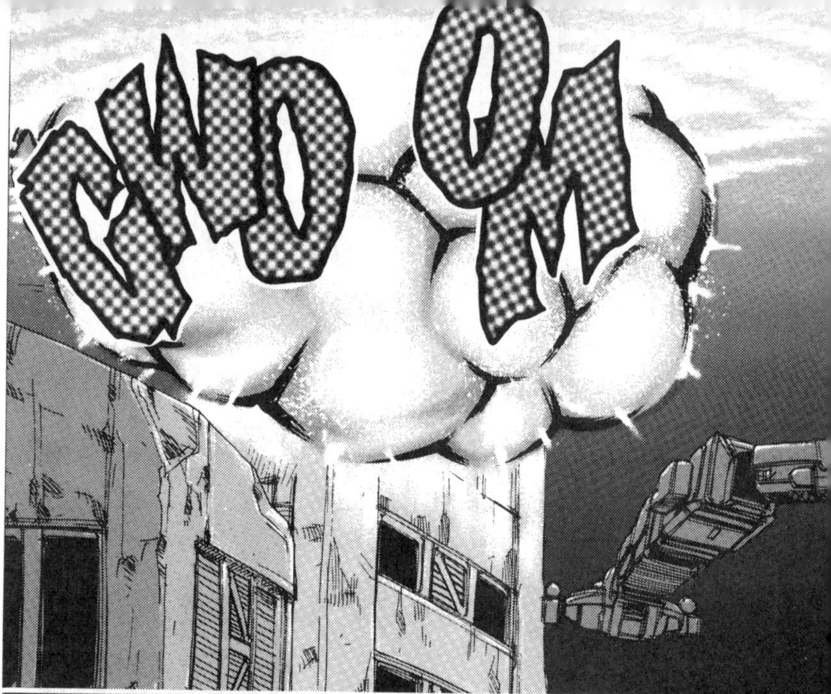

Battle at the Bottom of the Sea

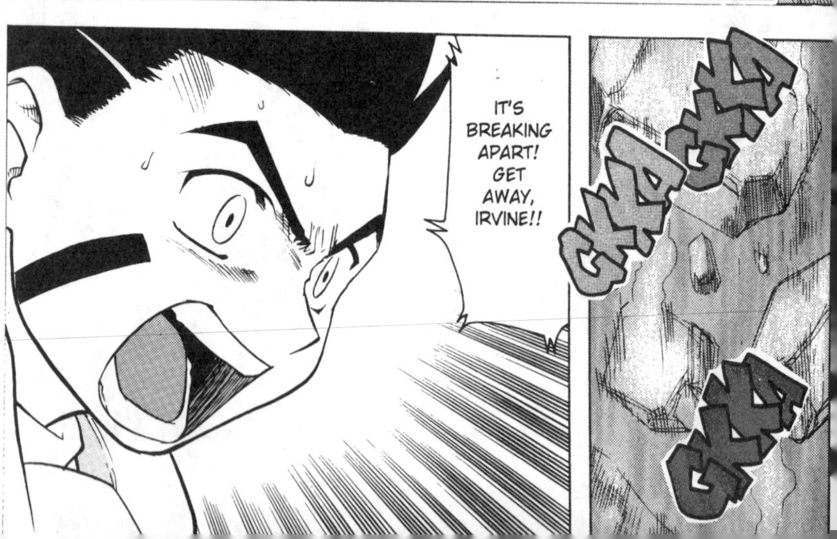
GKAGKA
GKA
IT'S BREAKING APART! GET AWAY, IRVINE!!

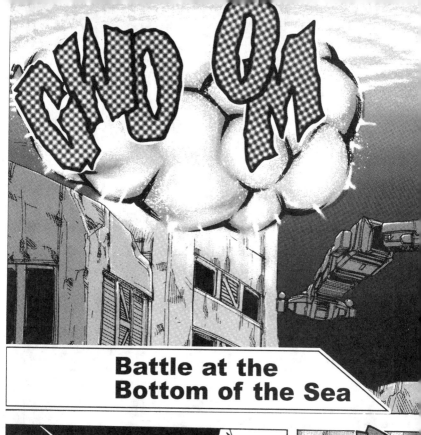

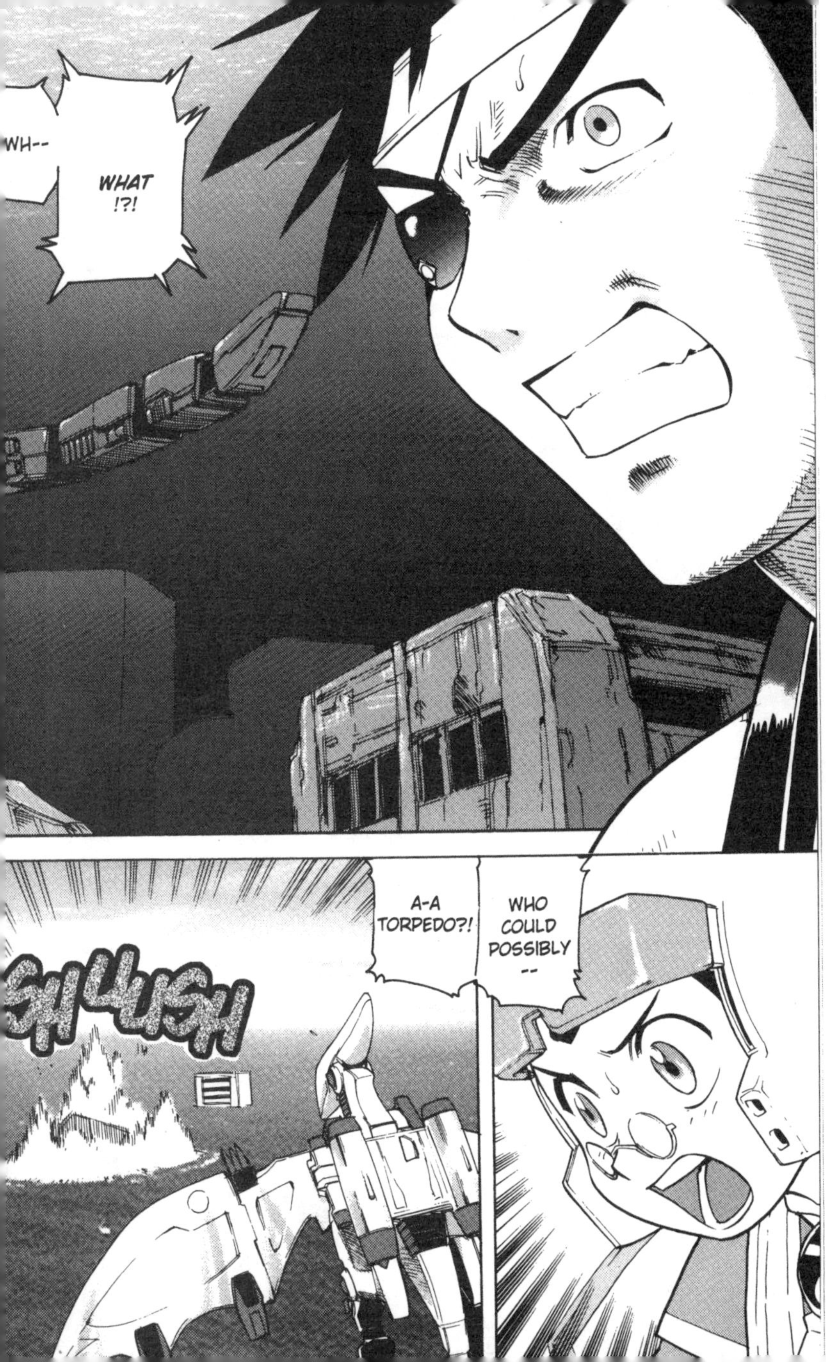
WH--
WHAT !?!
SHUUSH
A-A TORPEDO?!
WHO COULD POSSIBLY --

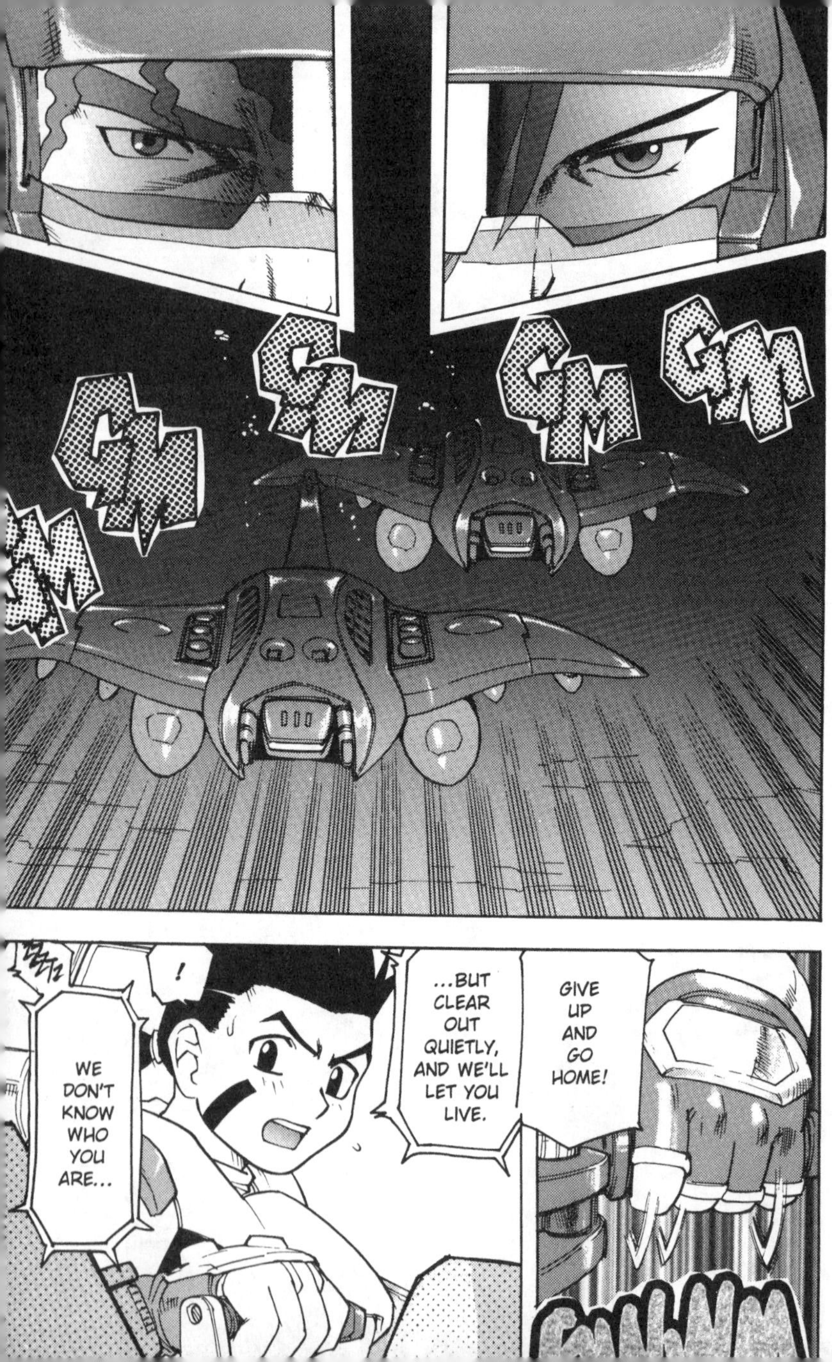
GM
GM
GM
GM
!
WE DON'T KNOW WHO YOU ARE...
...BUT CLEAR OUT QUIETLY, AND WE'LL LET YOU LIVE.
GIVE UP AND GO HOME!

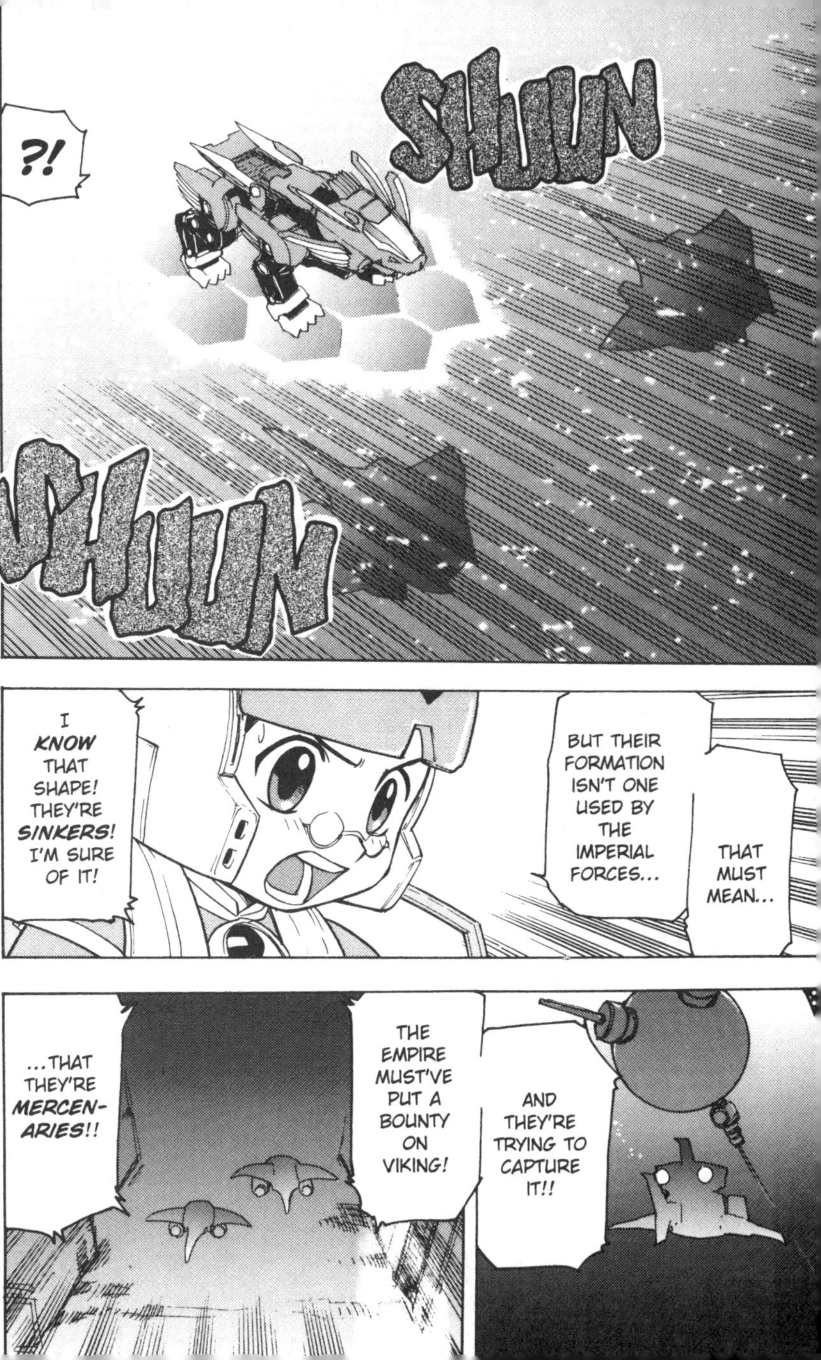

?!
SHUUN
SHUUN
I *KNOW* THAT SHAPE! THEY'RE *SINKERS*! I'M SURE OF IT!
BUT THEIR FORMATION ISN'T ONE USED BY THE IMPERIAL FORCES...
THAT MUST MEAN...
...THAT THEY'RE *MERCEN-ARIES*!!
THE EMPIRE MUST'VE PUT A BOUNTY ON VIKING!
AND THEY'RE TRYING TO CAPTURE IT!!

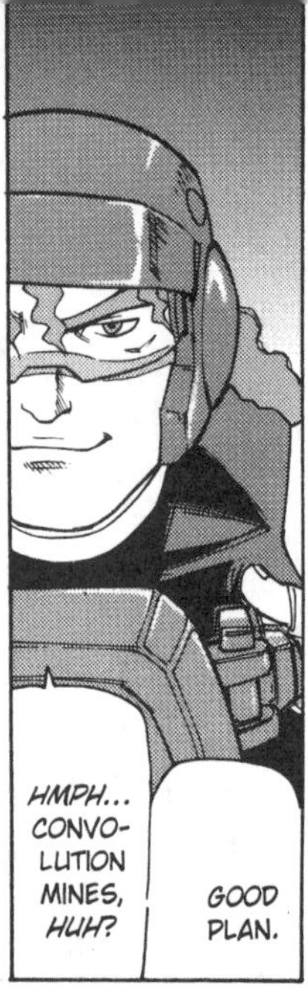
HMPH... CONVO-LUTION MINES, HUH?
GOOD PLAN.
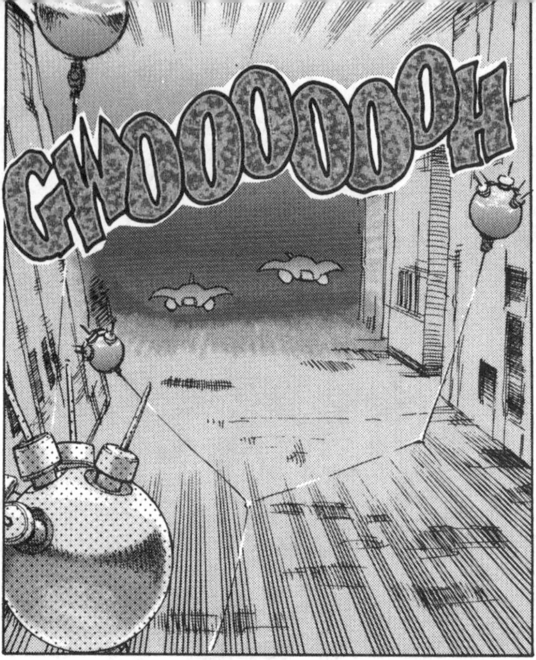
GWOOOOOOH
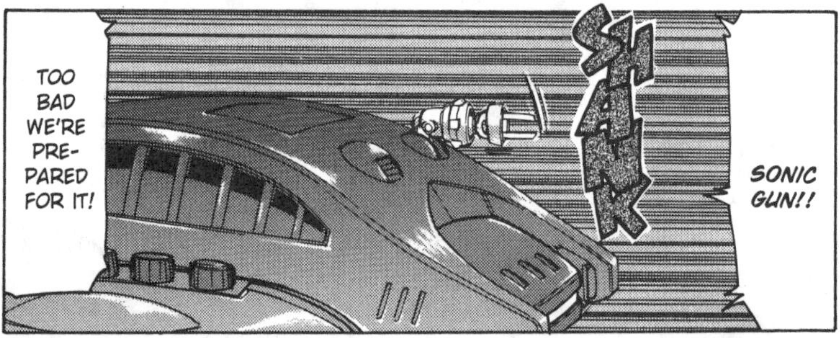
SONIC GUN!!
SHANK
TOO BAD WE'RE PRE-PARED FOR IT!
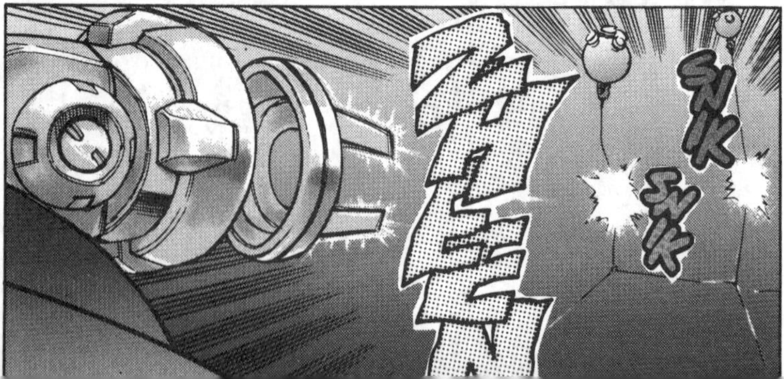
SNIK
SNIK

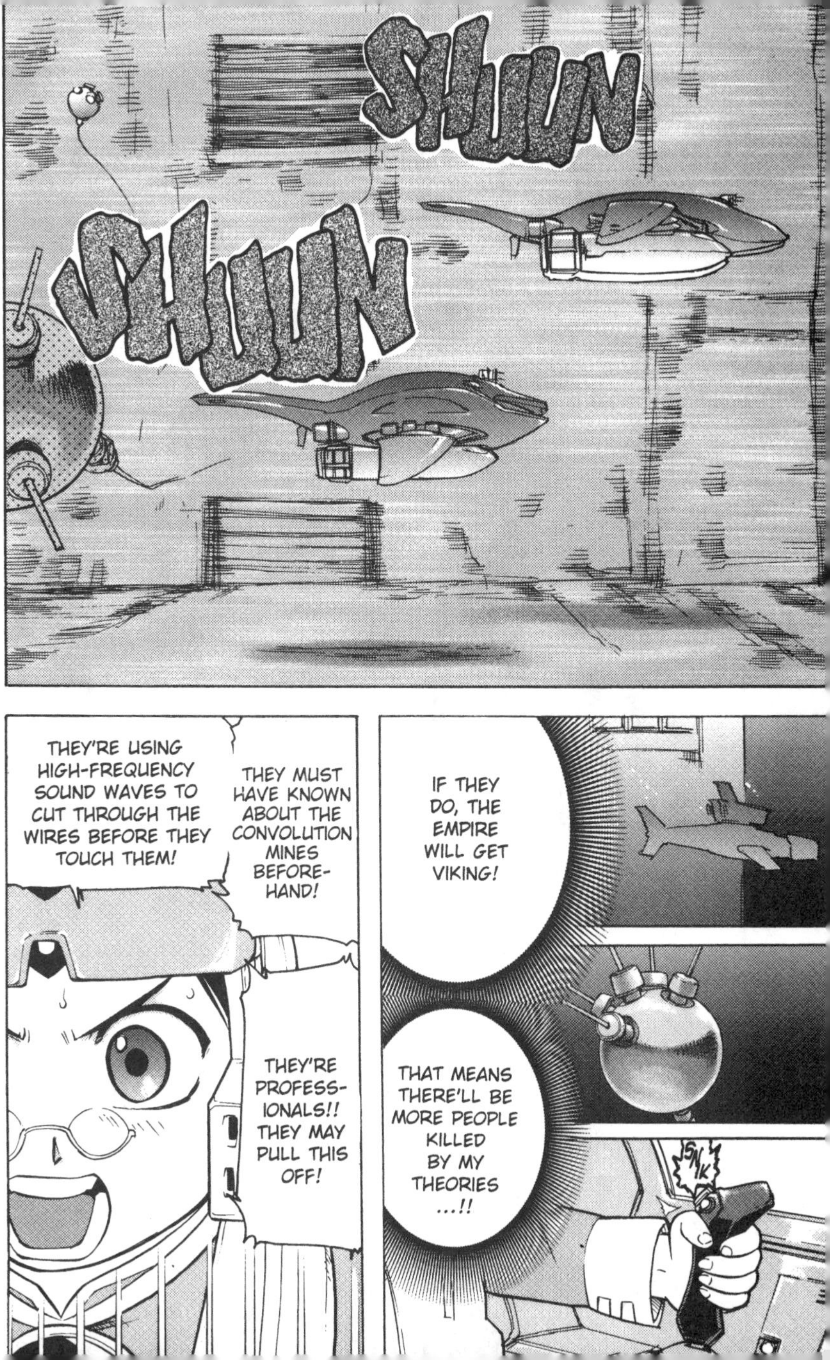
SHUUN
SHUUN
THEY'RE USING HIGH-FREQUENCY SOUND WAVES TO CUT THROUGH THE WIRES BEFORE THEY TOUCH THEM!
THEY MUST HAVE KNOWN ABOUT THE CONVOLUTION MINES BEFORE-HAND!
THEY'RE PROFESS-IONALS!! THEY MAY PULL THIS OFF!
IF THEY DO, THE EMPIRE WILL GET VIKING!
THAT MEANS THERE'LL BE MORE PEOPLE KILLED BY MY THEORIES ...!!
SNIK

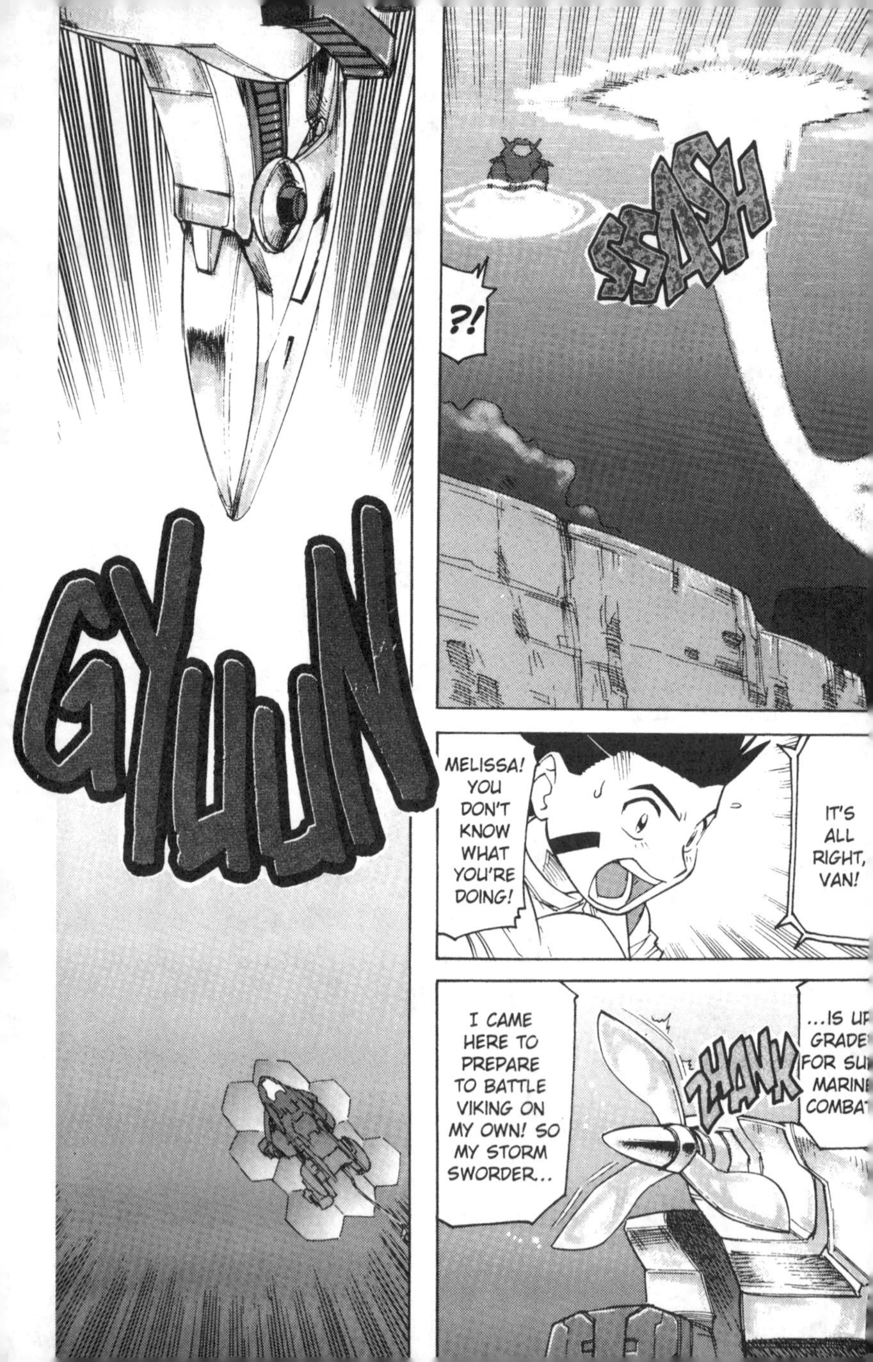
GYUUUN
SSASH
?!
MELISSA! YOU DON'T KNOW WHAT YOU'RE DOING!
IT'S ALL RIGHT, VAN!
I CAME HERE TO PREPARE TO BATTLE VIKING ON MY OWN! SO MY STORM SWORDER...
ZHANK
...IS UP
GRADE
FOR SU
MARINE
COMBAT

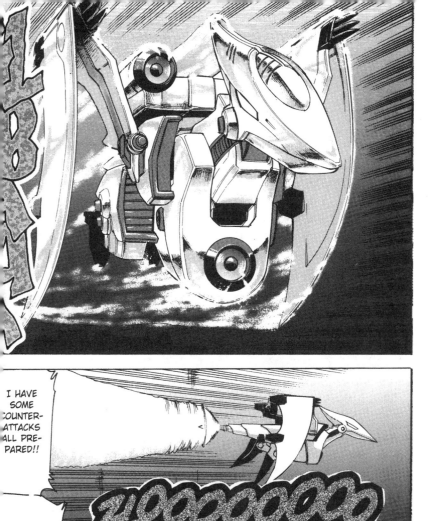

I HAVE SOME COUNTER-ATTACKS ALL PRE-PARED!!

ZUOOOOOOOOOO

SO VAN, YOUR JOB IS TO *HELP IRVINE!*

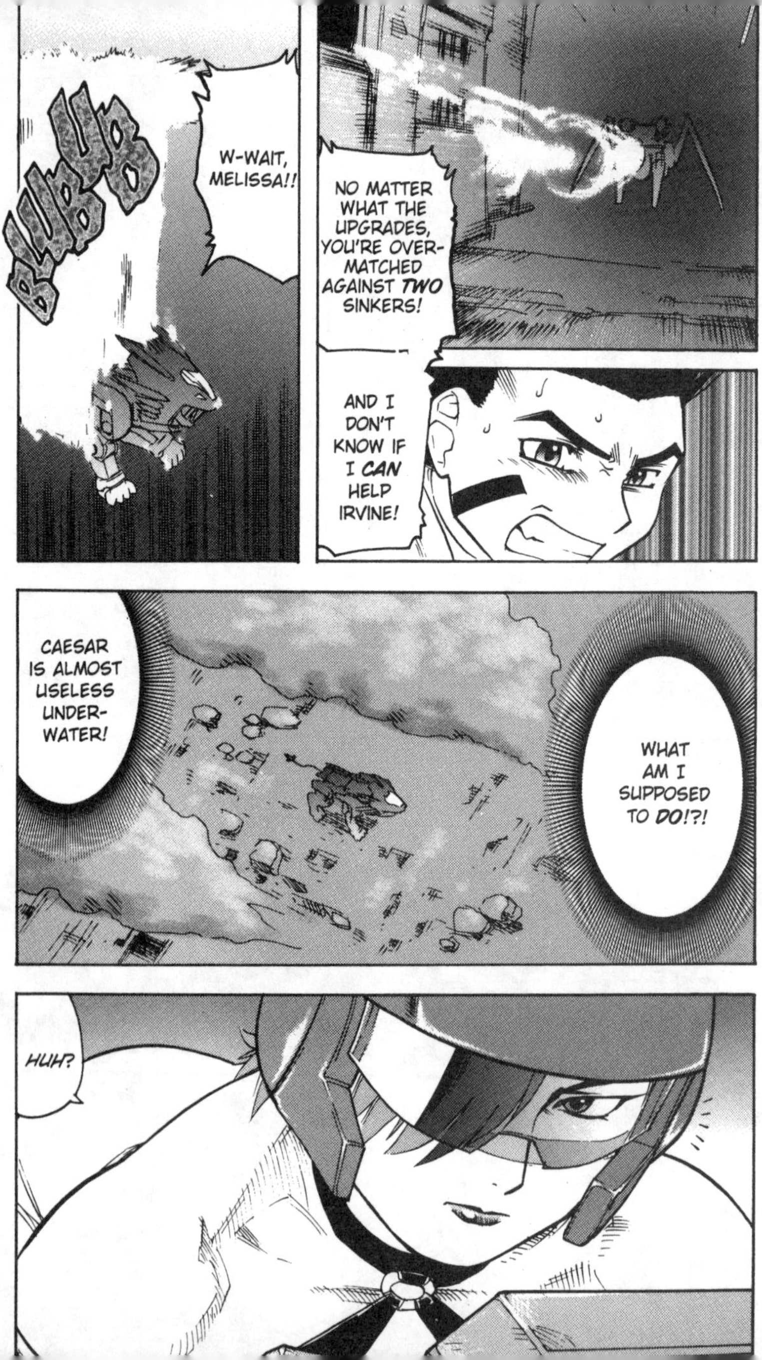
BLUBUB
W-WAIT, MELISSA!!
NO MATTER WHAT THE UPGRADES, YOU'RE OVER-MATCHED AGAINST *TWO* SINKERS!
AND I DON'T KNOW IF I *CAN* HELP IRVINE!
CAESAR IS ALMOST USELESS UNDER-WATER!
WHAT AM I SUPPOSED TO *DO*!?!
HUH?

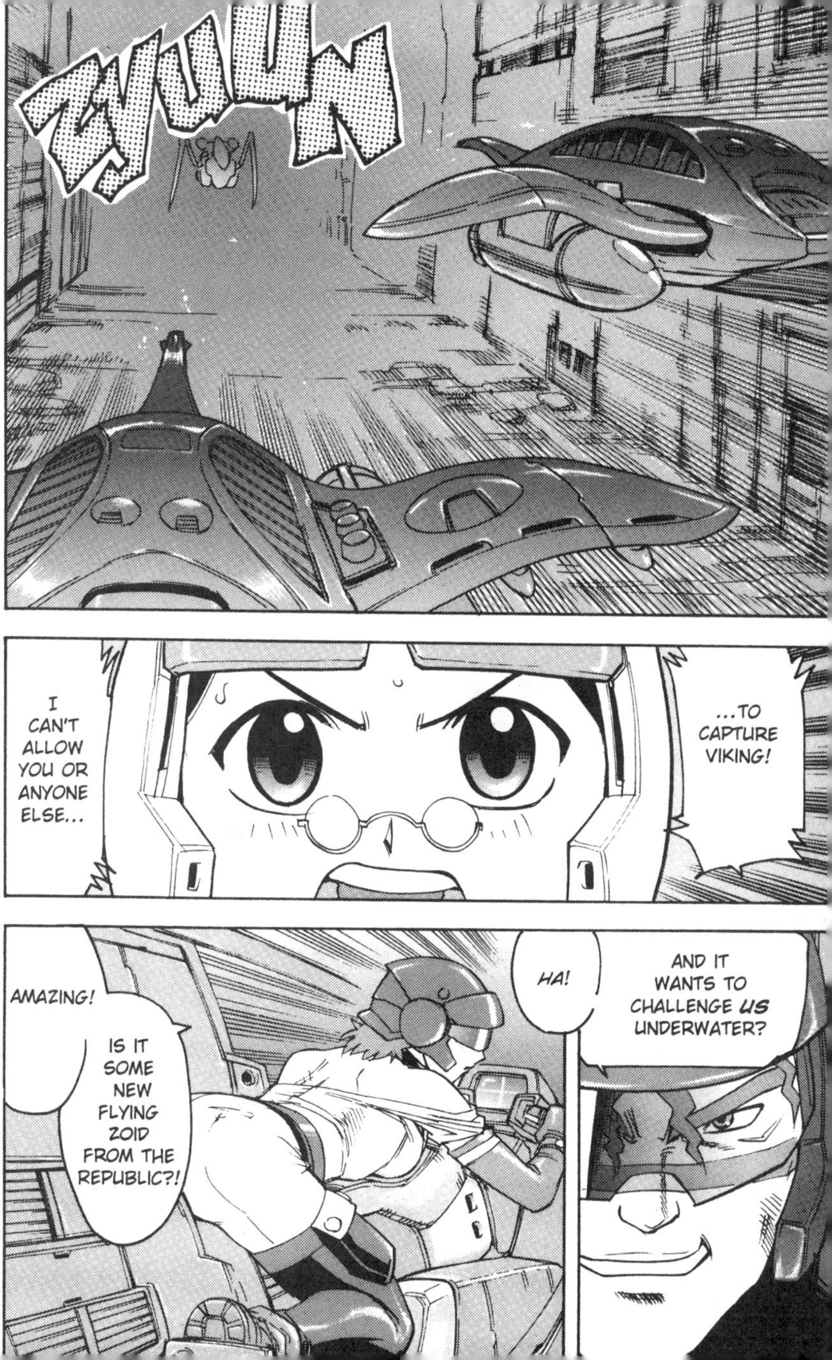
ZYUUN
I CAN'T ALLOW YOU OR ANYONE ELSE...
...TO CAPTURE VIKING!
AMAZING!
IS IT SOME NEW FLYING ZOID FROM THE REPUBLIC?!
HA!
AND IT WANTS TO CHALLENGE *US* UNDERWATER?

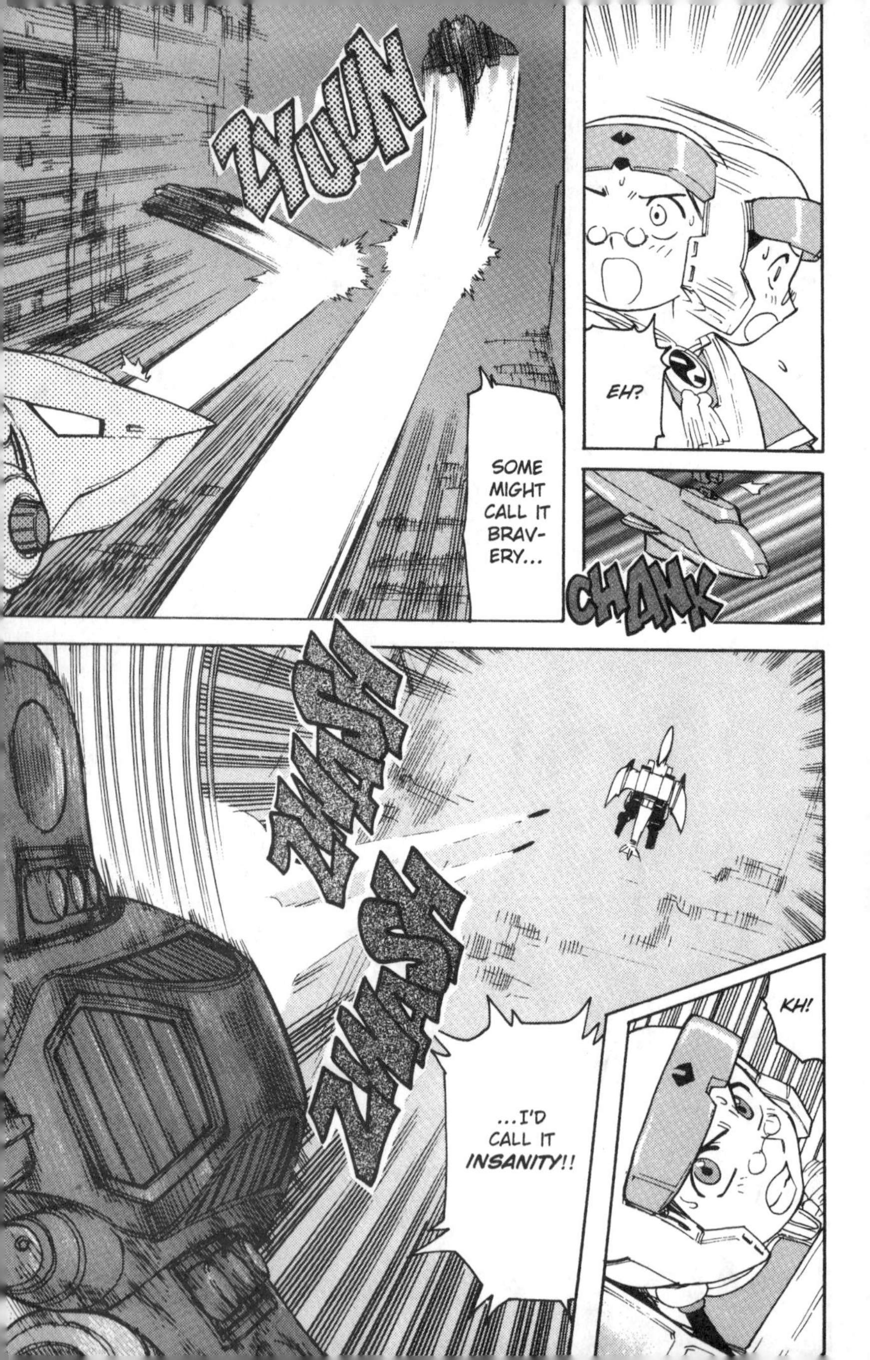
EH?
CHANK
ZKUUN
SOME MIGHT CALL IT BRAVERY...
ZWASH
ZWASH
KH!
...I'D CALL IT *INSANITY*!!

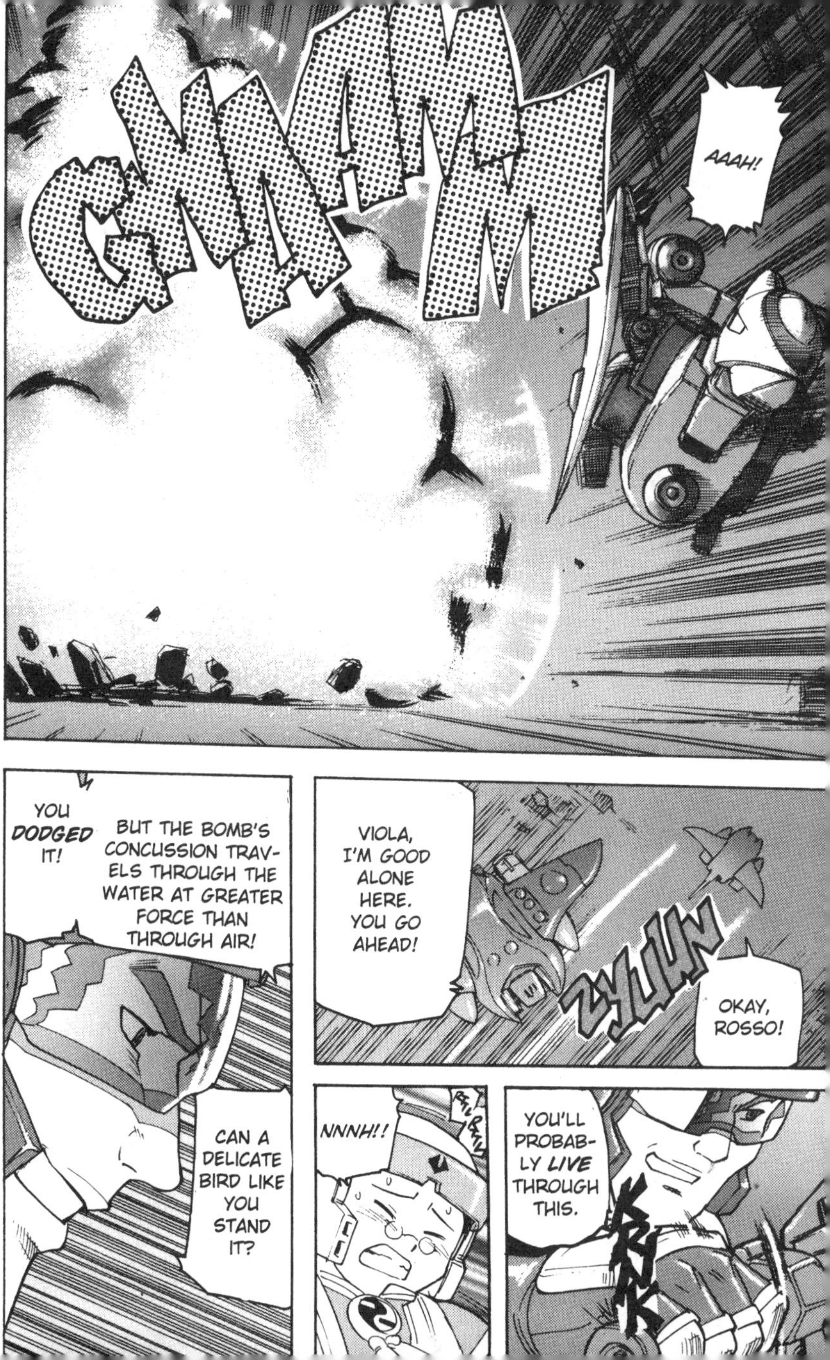
AAAH!
VIOLA, I'M GOOD ALONE HERE. YOU GO AHEAD!
ZYUUN
OKAY, ROSSO!
YOU *DODGED* IT!
BUT THE BOMB'S CONCUSSION TRAV-ELS THROUGH THE WATER AT GREATER FORCE THAN THROUGH AIR!
CAN A DELICATE BIRD LIKE YOU STAND IT?
NNNH!!
YOU'LL PROBAB-LY *LIVE* THROUGH THIS.

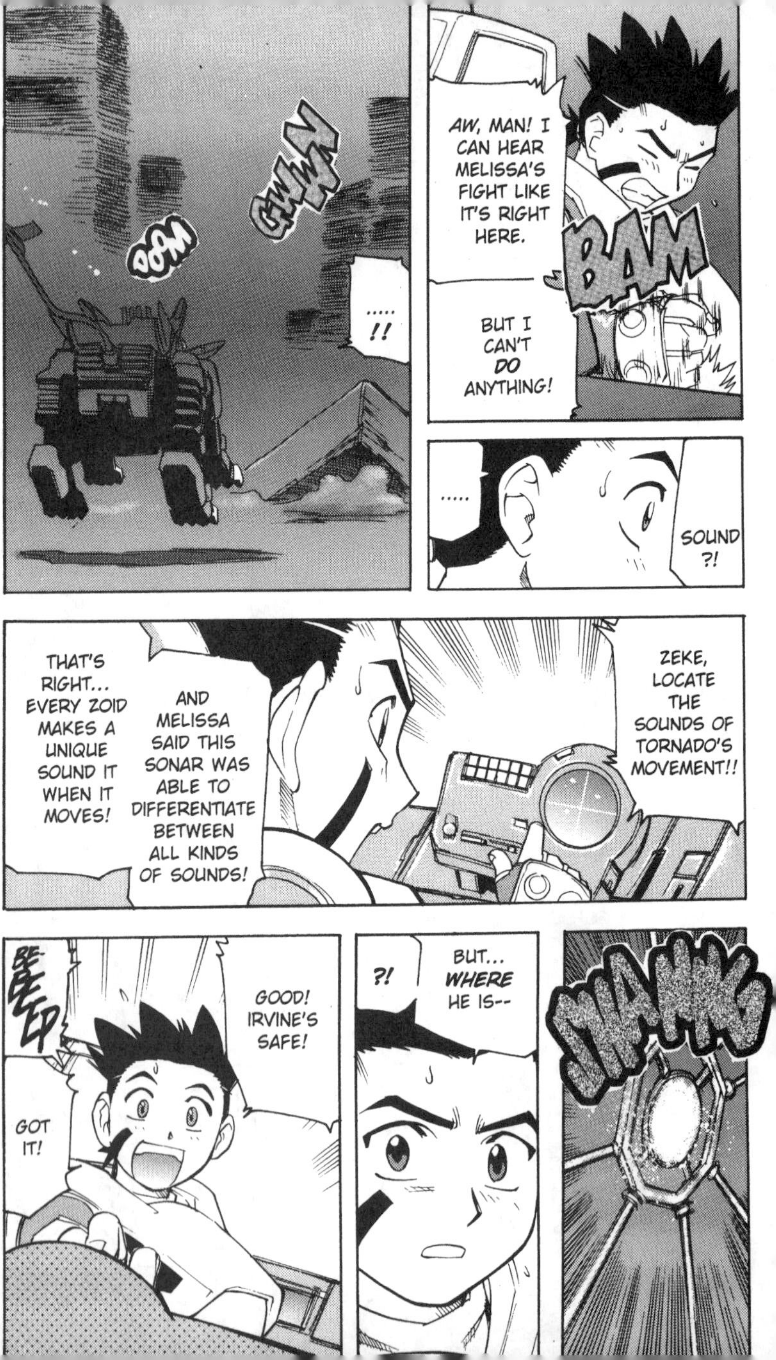
AW, MAN! I CAN HEAR MELISSA'S FIGHT LIKE IT'S RIGHT HERE.
BAM
BUT I CAN'T *DO* ANYTHING!
.....
SOUND ?!
..... !!
ZEKE, LOCATE THE SOUNDS OF TORNADO'S MOVEMENT!!
AND MELISSA SAID THIS SONAR WAS ABLE TO DIFFERENTIATE BETWEEN ALL KINDS OF SOUNDS!
THAT'S RIGHT... EVERY ZOID MAKES A UNIQUE SOUND IT WHEN IT MOVES!
BUT... ***WHERE*** HE IS--
?!
GOOD! IRVINE'S SAFE!
GOT IT!
BE-BEEP

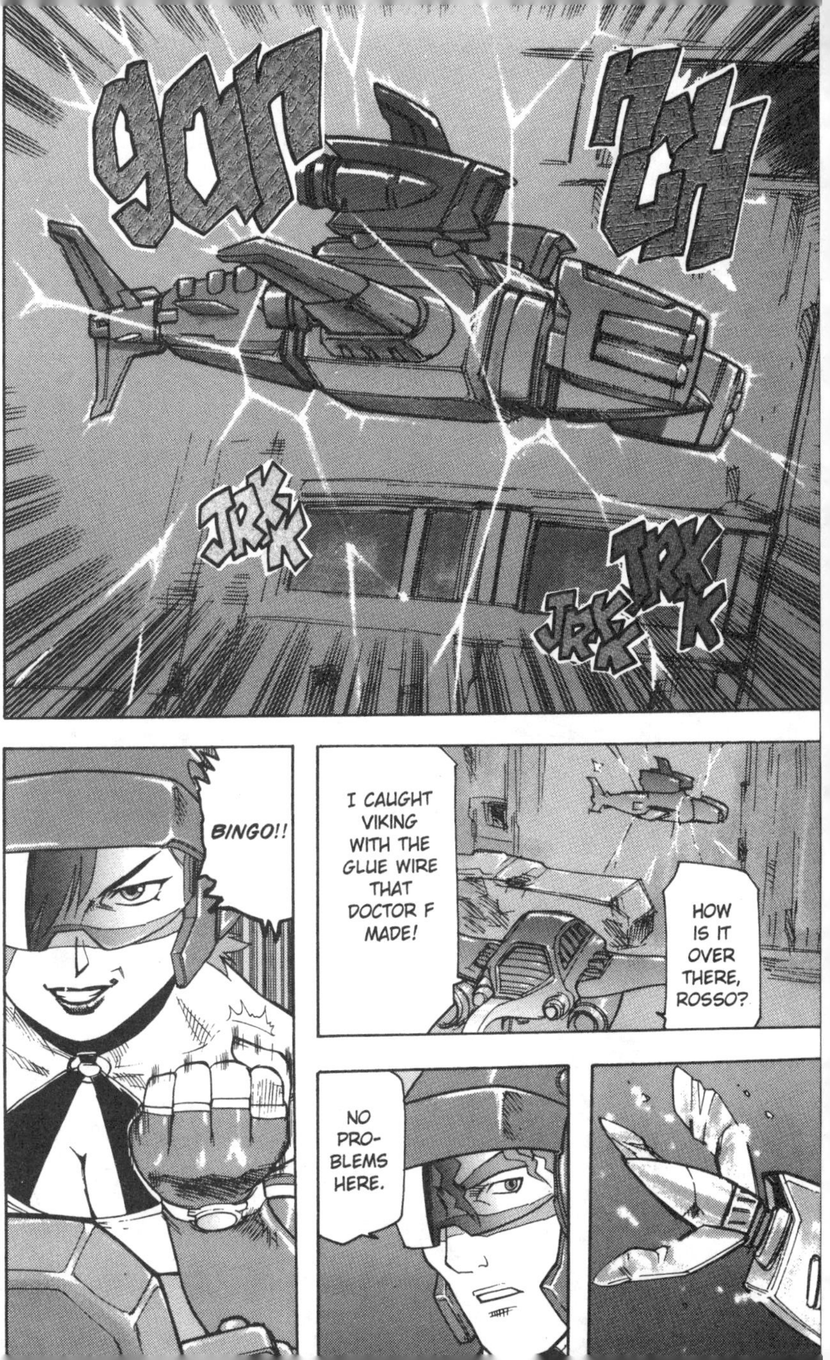
NCH
gon
JRKK
JRKK
JRKK
I CAUGHT VIKING WITH THE GLUE WIRE THAT DOCTOR F MADE!
HOW IS IT OVER THERE, ROSSO?
NO PRO-BLEMS HERE.
BINGO!!

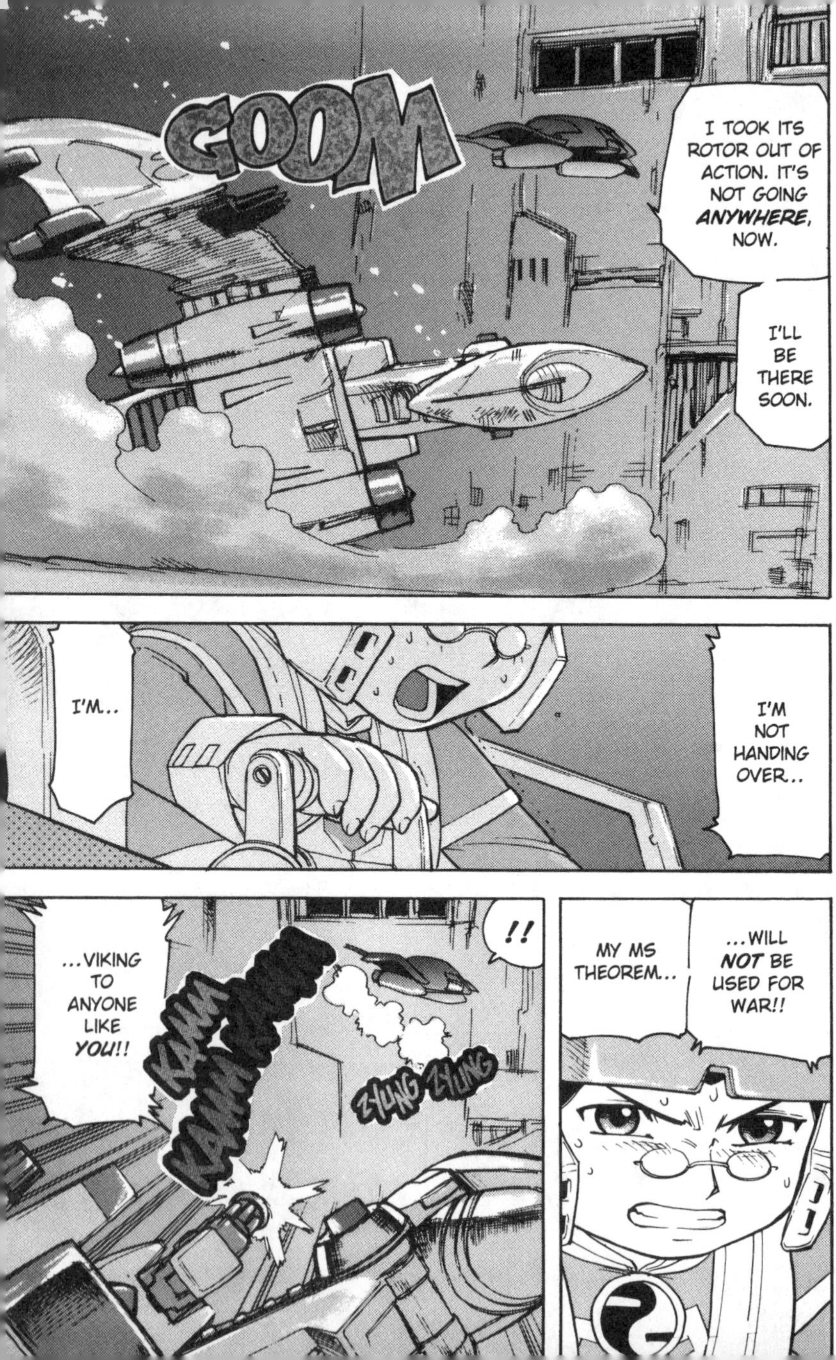
I TOOK ITS ROTOR OUT OF ACTION. IT'S NOT GOING ***ANYWHERE***, NOW.
I'LL BE THERE SOON.
GOOM
I'M...
I'M NOT HANDING OVER...
...VIKING TO ANYONE LIKE ***YOU***!!
!!
KAWM KAWM
ZYUNG ZYUNG
MY MS THEOREM...
...WILL ***NOT*** BE USED FOR WAR!!

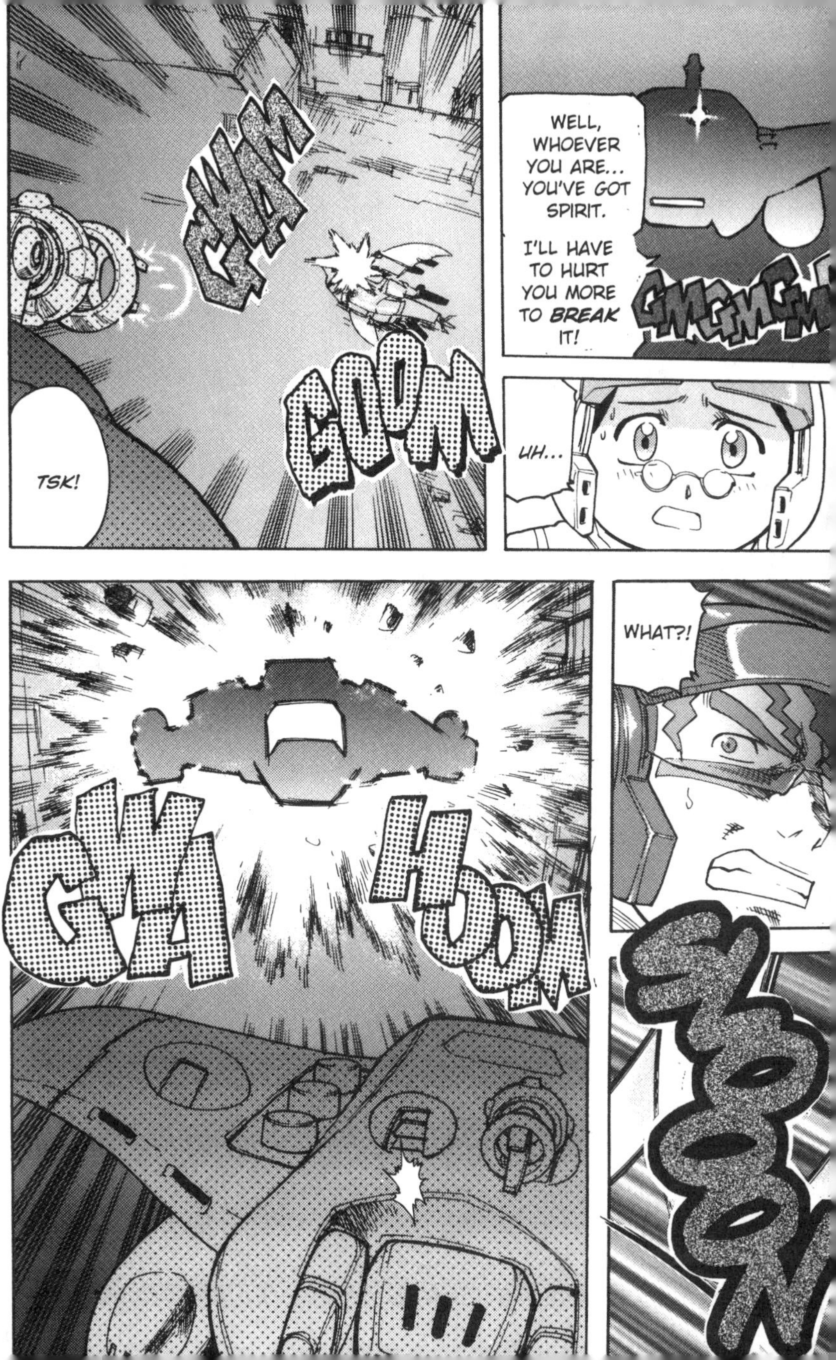
WELL, WHOEVER YOU ARE... YOU'VE GOT SPIRIT.
I'LL HAVE TO HURT YOU MORE TO *BREAK* IT!
GMGMGMGM
UH...
GWAM
GOOM
TSK!
WHAT?!
SHOOOON
GWA HOOM

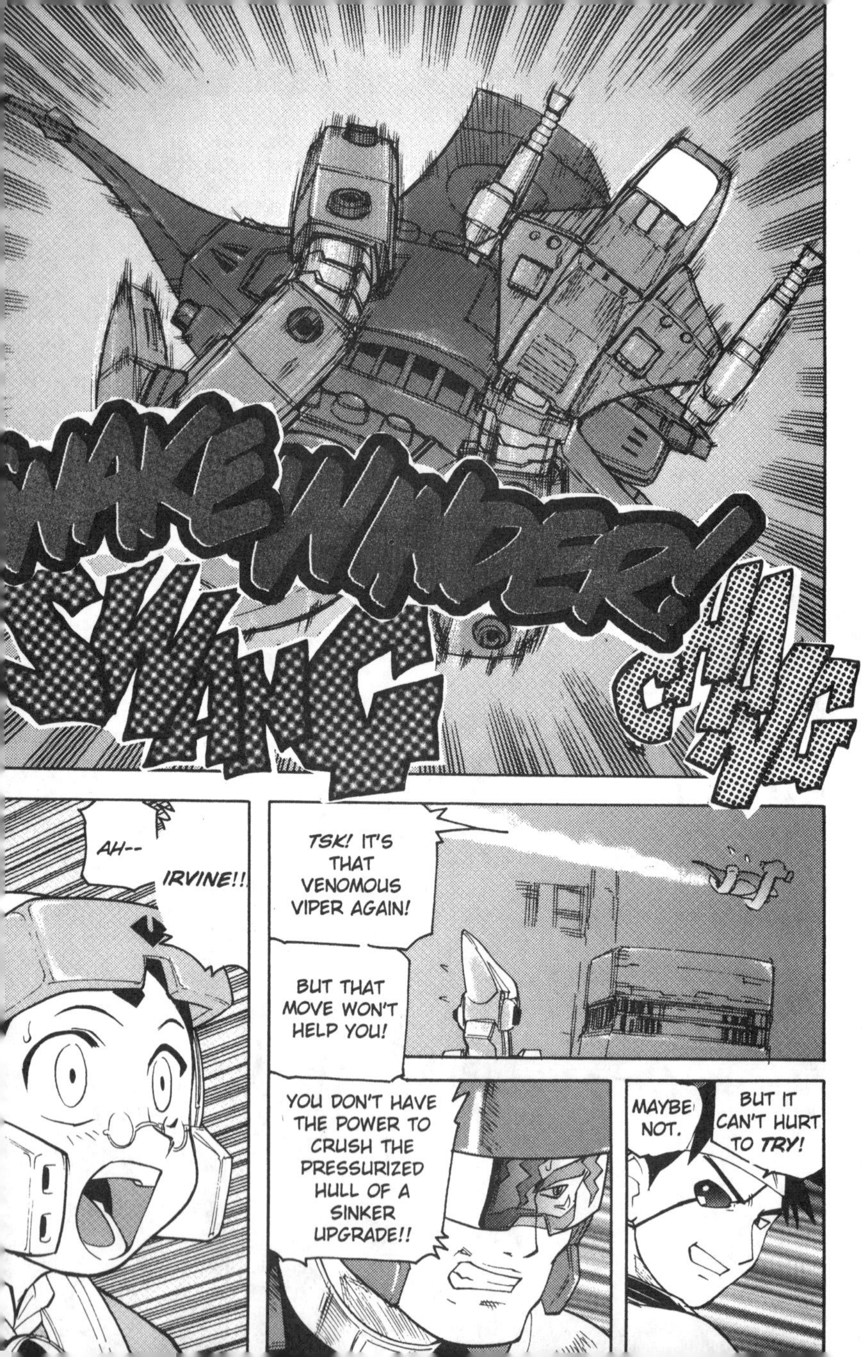
AH--
IRVINE!!
TSK! IT'S THAT VENOMOUS VIPER AGAIN!
BUT THAT MOVE WON'T HELP YOU!
YOU DON'T HAVE THE POWER TO CRUSH THE PRESSURIZED HULL OF A SINKER UPGRADE!!
MAYBE NOT.
BUT IT CAN'T HURT TO TRY!

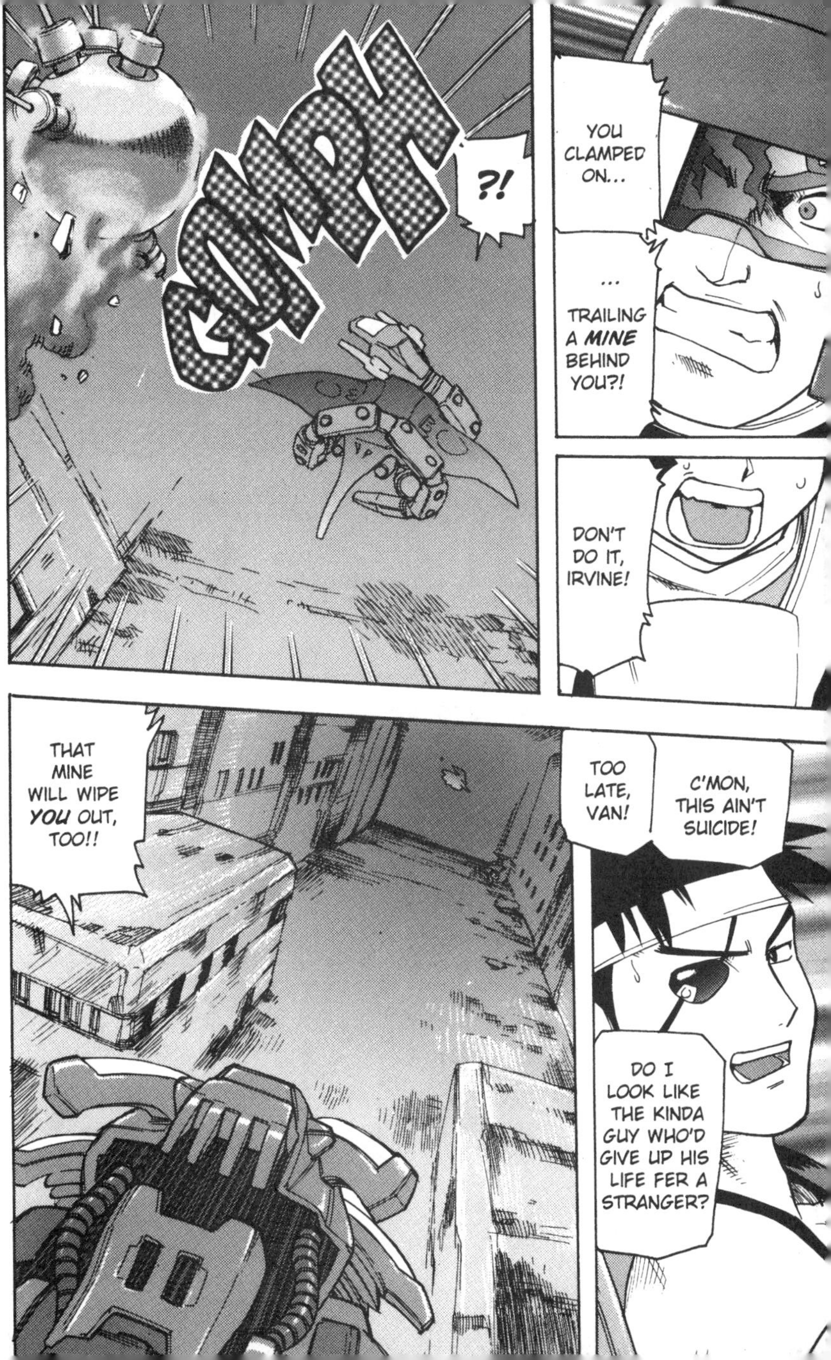
YOU CLAMPED ON...
... TRAILING A *MINE* BEHIND YOU?!
DON'T DO IT, IRVINE!
?!
TOO LATE, VAN!
C'MON, THIS AIN'T SUICIDE!
DO I LOOK LIKE THE KINDA GUY WHO'D GIVE UP HIS LIFE FER A STRANGER?
THAT MINE WILL WIPE *YOU* OUT, TOO!!

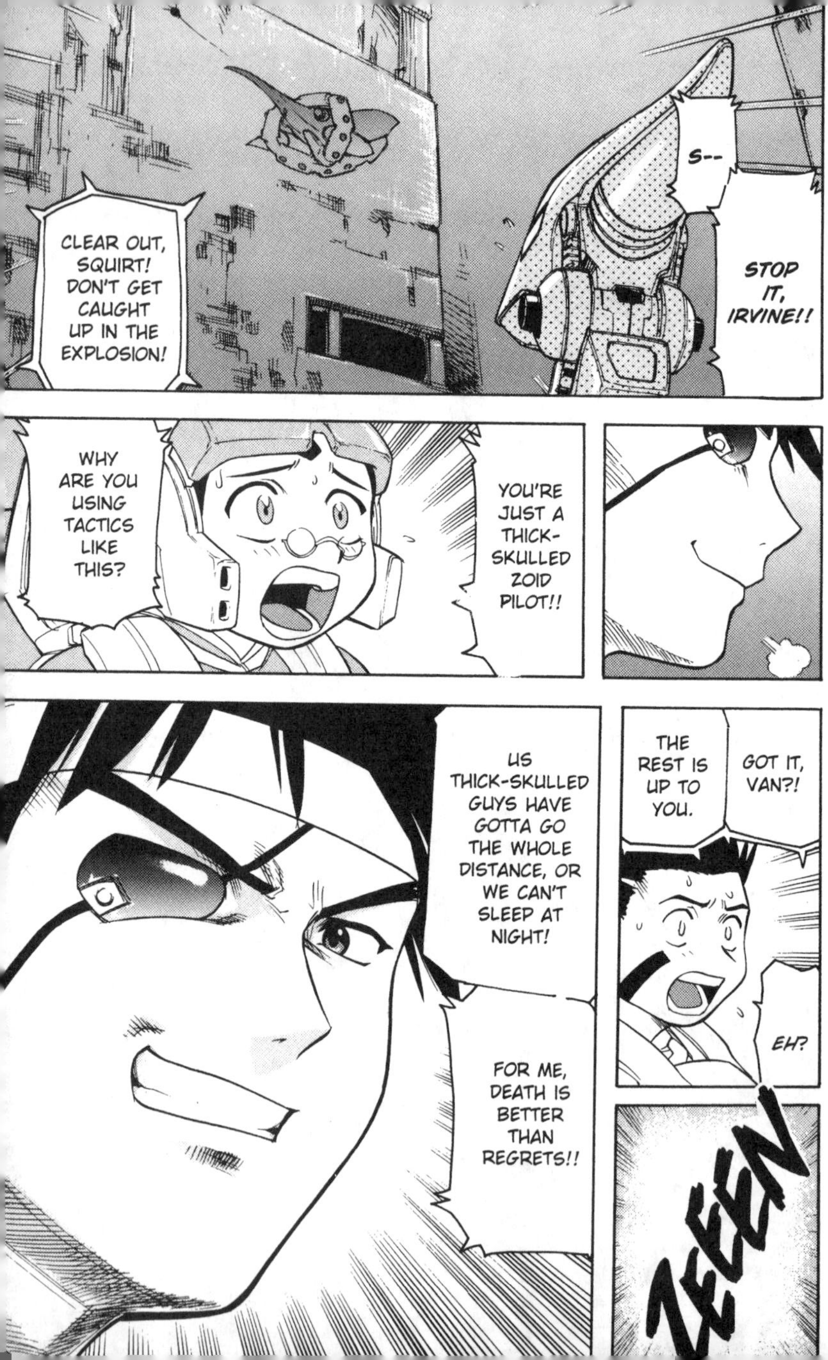
CLEAR OUT, SQUIRT! DON'T GET CAUGHT UP IN THE EXPLOSION!
S--
STOP IT, IRVINE!!
WHY ARE YOU USING TACTICS LIKE THIS?
YOU'RE JUST A THICK-SKULLED ZOID PILOT!!
US THICK-SKULLED GUYS HAVE GOTTA GO THE WHOLE DISTANCE, OR WE CAN'T SLEEP AT NIGHT!
FOR ME, DEATH IS BETTER THAN REGRETS!!
THE REST IS UP TO YOU.
GOT IT, VAN?!
EH?
ZEEEN

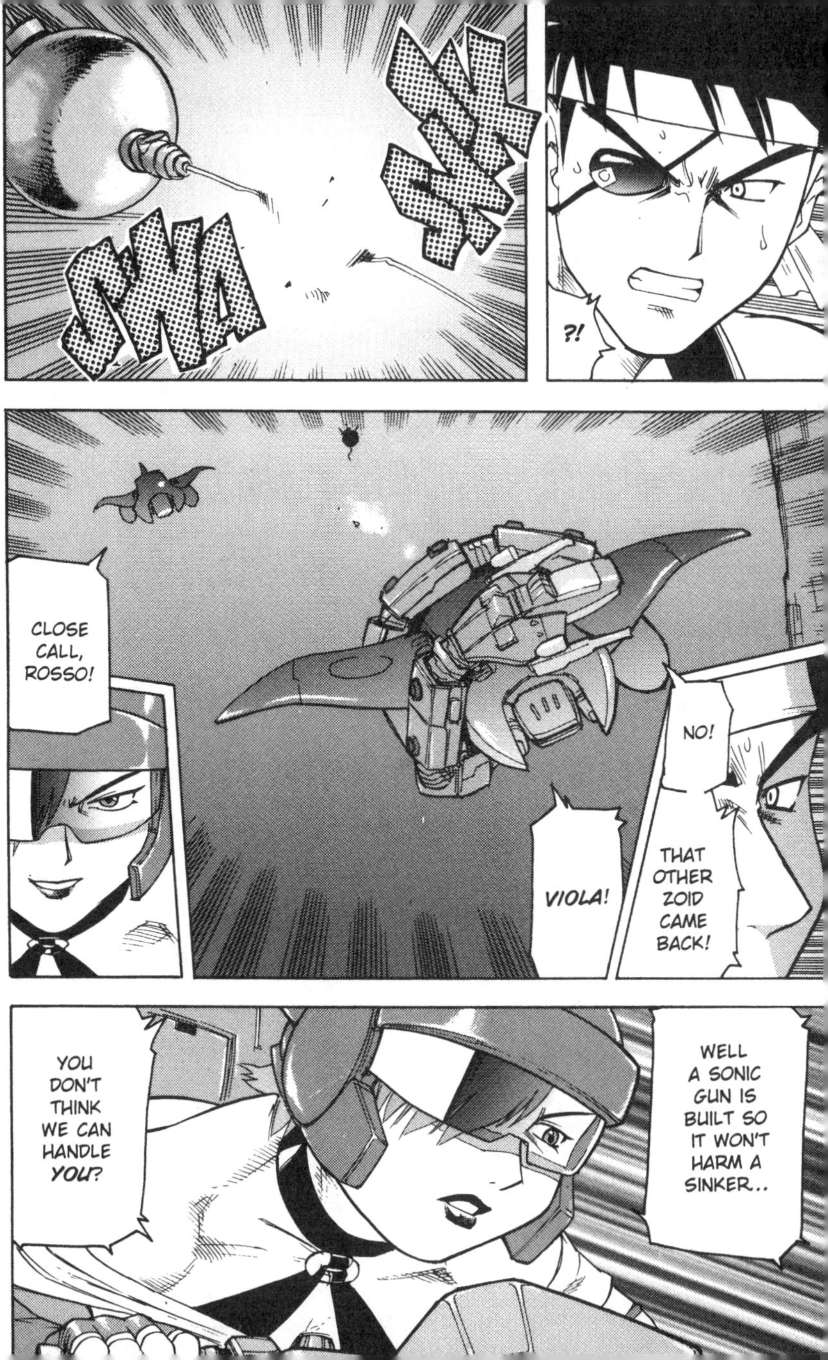
?!
SWA
NO!
THAT OTHER ZOID CAME BACK!
VIOLA!
CLOSE CALL, ROSSO!
WELL A SONIC GUN IS BUILT SO IT WON'T HARM A SINKER..
YOU DON'T THINK WE CAN HANDLE *YOU*?

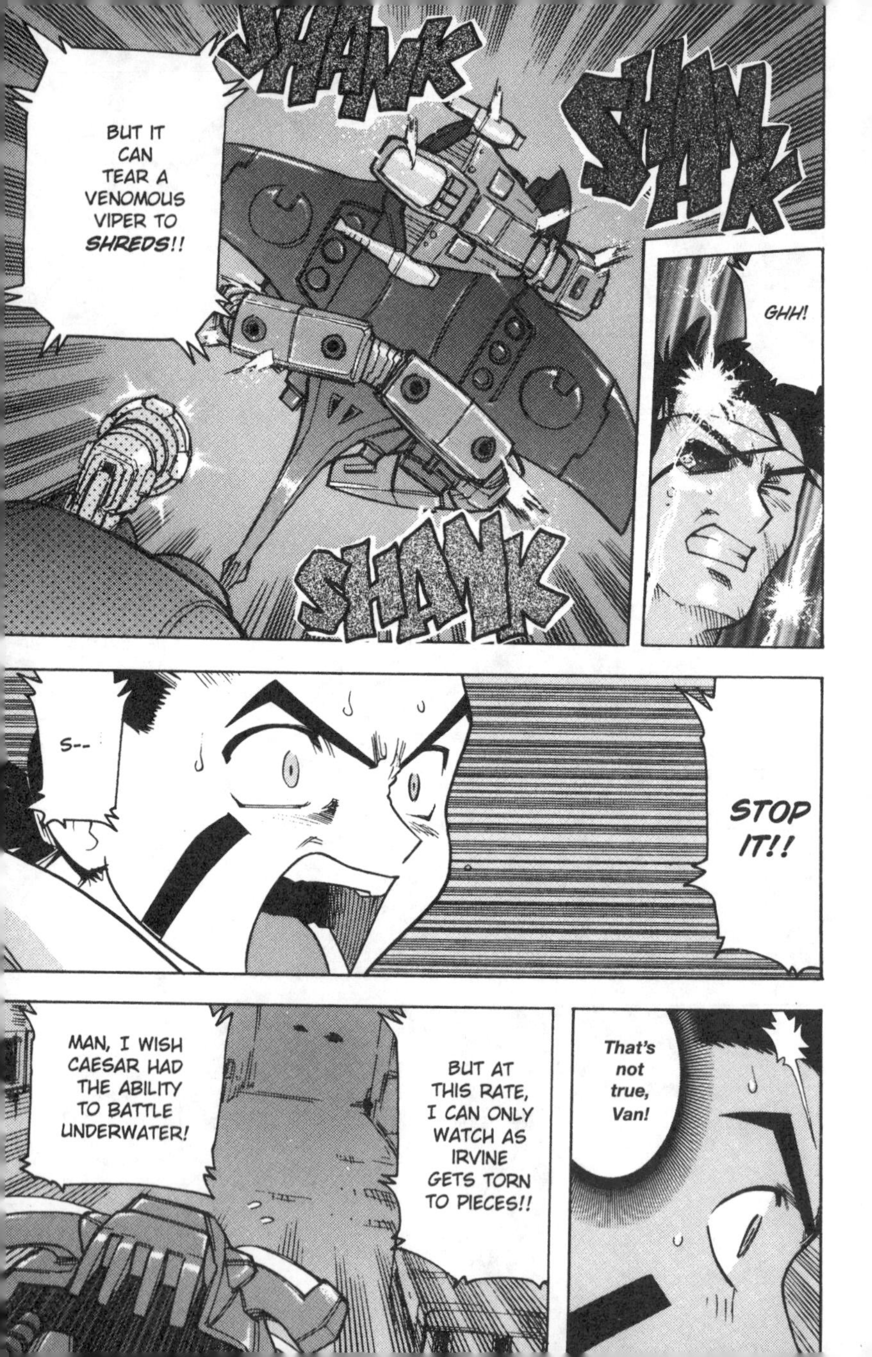
BUT IT CAN TEAR A VENOMOUS VIPER TO SHREDS!!
SHANK
SHANK
SHANK
GHH!
S--
STOP IT!!
MAN, I WISH CAESAR HAD THE ABILITY TO BATTLE UNDERWATER!
BUT AT THIS RATE, I CAN ONLY WATCH AS IRVINE GETS TORN TO PIECES!!
That's not true, Van!

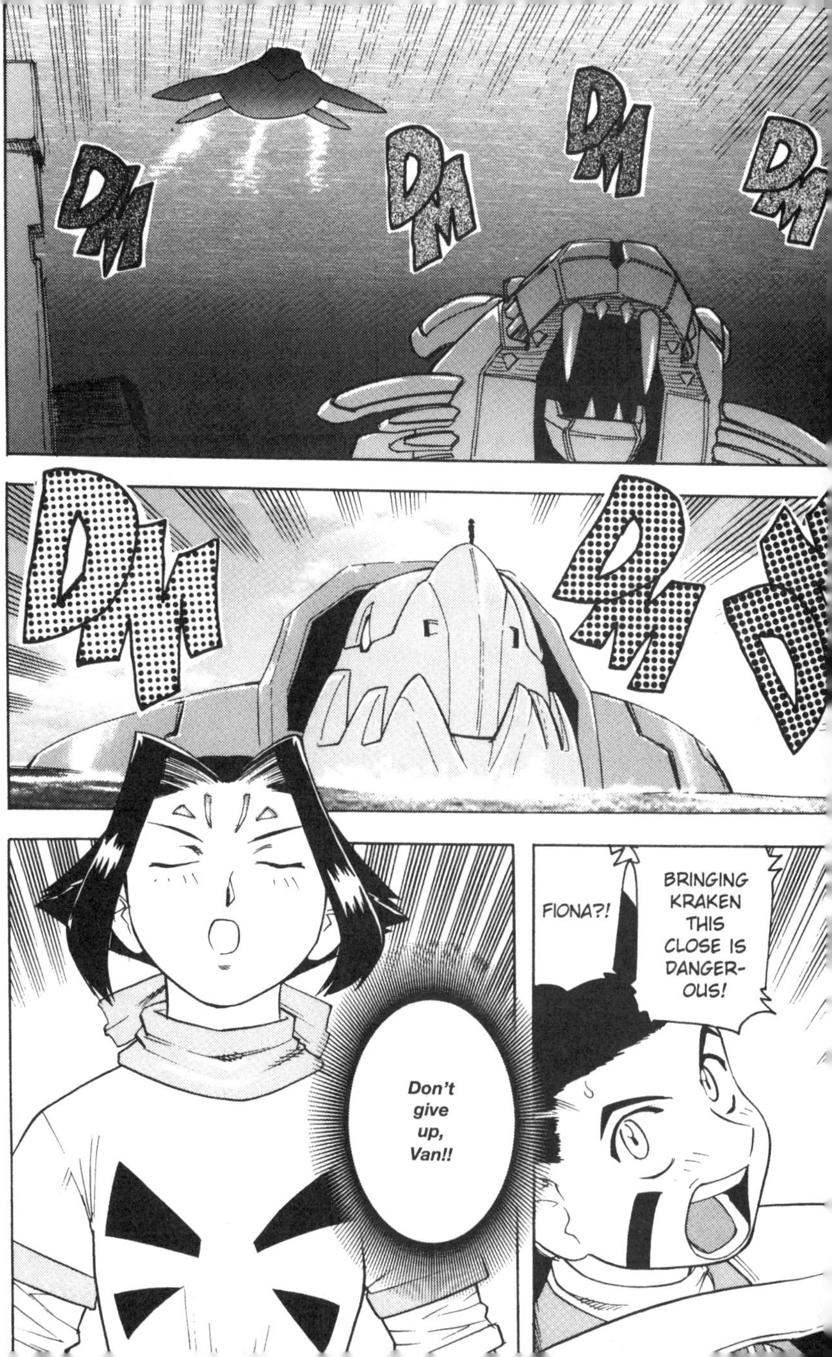
DM
DM
DM
DM
DM
DM
BRINGING KRAKEN THIS CLOSE IS DANGER-OUS!
FIONA?!
Don't give up, Van!!

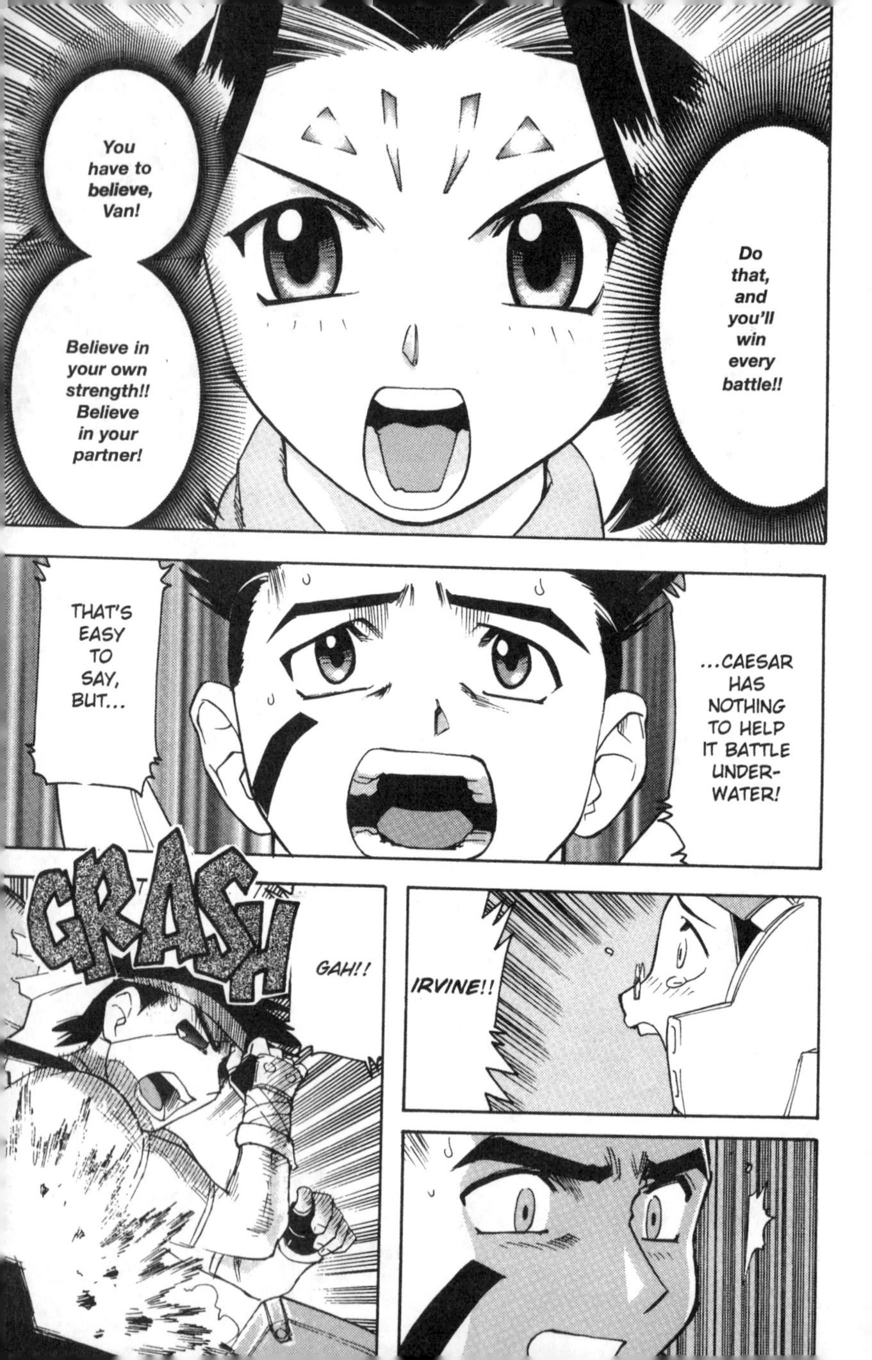
You have to believe, Van!
Believe in your own strength!! Believe in your partner!
Do that, and you'll win every battle!!
THAT'S EASY TO SAY, BUT...
...CAESAR HAS NOTHING TO HELP IT BATTLE UNDER-WATER!
GRASH
GAH!!
IRVINE!!

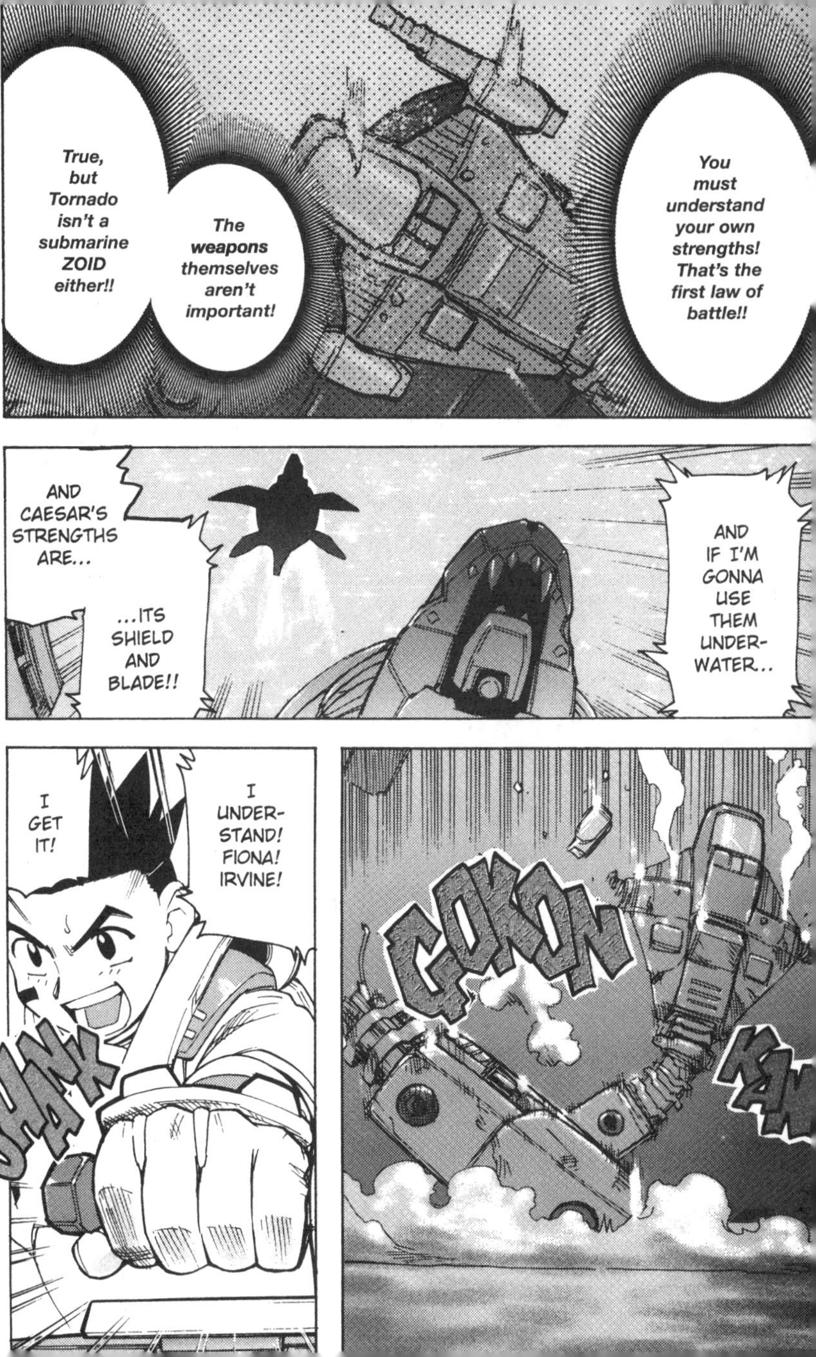
You must understand your own strengths! That's the first law of battle!!
The weapons themselves aren't important!
True, but Tornado isn't a submarine ZOID either!!
AND CAESAR'S STRENGTHS ARE...
...ITS SHIELD AND BLADE!!
AND IF I'M GONNA USE THEM UNDERWATER...
KAN
COKON
I UNDERSTAND! FIONA! IRVINE!
I GET IT!
SHAK

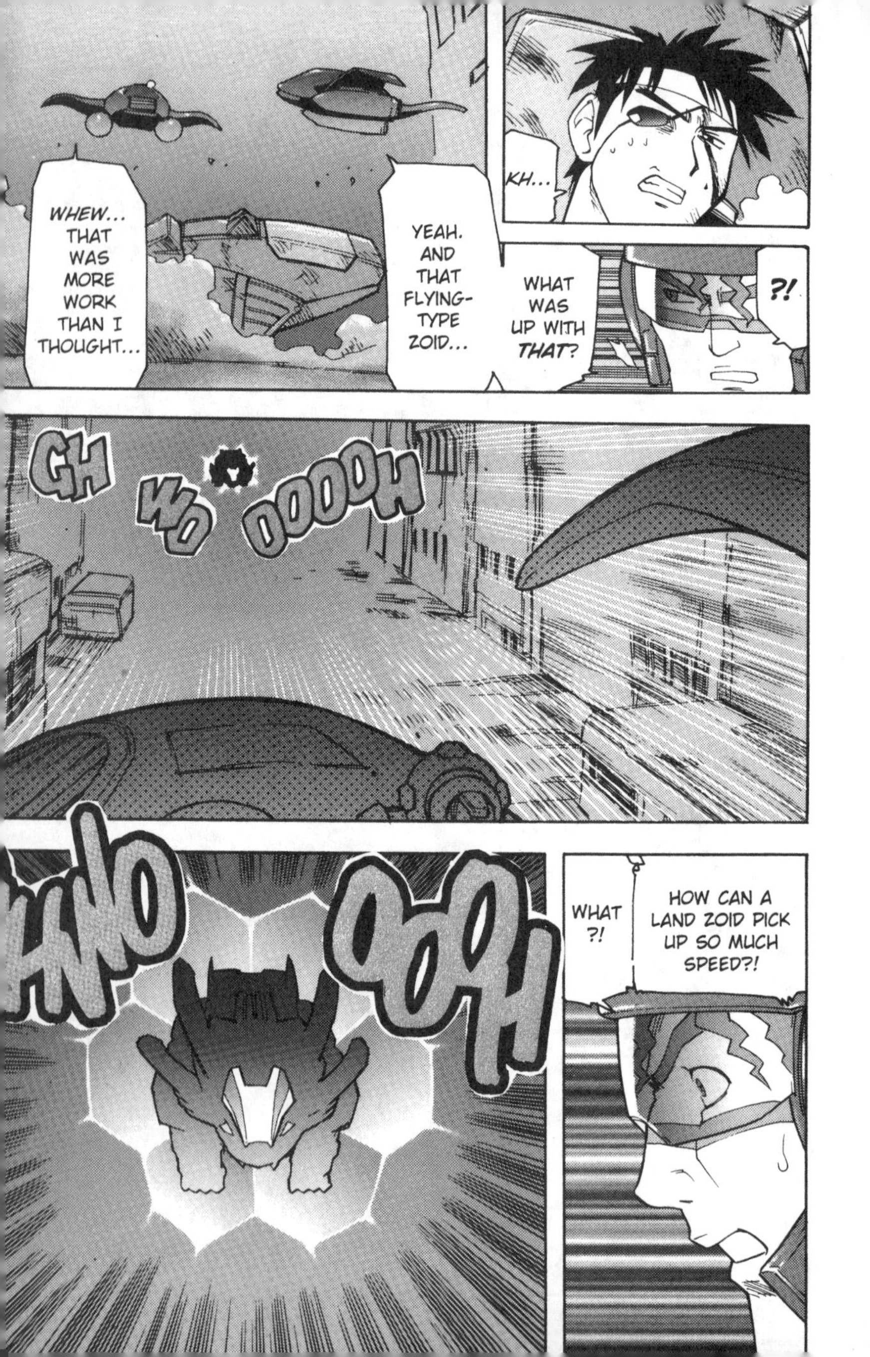
WHEW... THAT WAS MORE WORK THAN I THOUGHT...
YEAH. AND THAT FLYING-TYPE ZOID...
WHAT WAS UP WITH *THAT*?
KH...
?!
GH WO OOOOH
WHAT ?!
HOW CAN A LAND ZOID PICK UP SO MUCH SPEED?!
WO OOOH

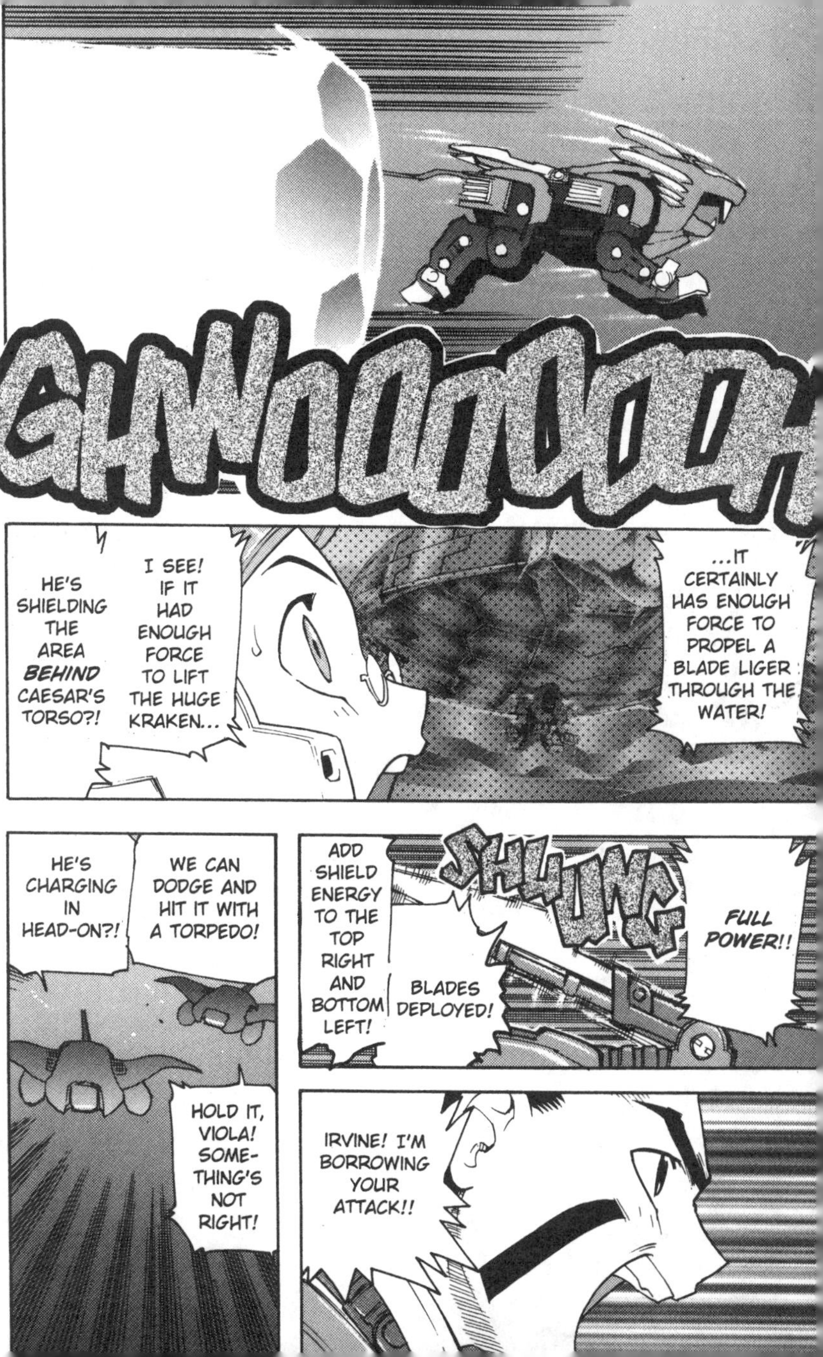
GHWOOOOOOH
...IT CERTAINLY HAS ENOUGH FORCE TO PROPEL A BLADE LIGER THROUGH THE WATER!
I SEE! IF IT HAD ENOUGH FORCE TO LIFT THE HUGE KRAKEN...
HE'S SHIELDING THE AREA *BEHIND* CAESAR'S TORSO?!
FULL POWER!!
SHLUNG
ADD SHIELD ENERGY TO THE TOP RIGHT AND BOTTOM LEFT!
BLADES DEPLOYED!
IRVINE! I'M BORROWING YOUR ATTACK!!
WE CAN DODGE AND HIT IT WITH A TORPEDO!
HE'S CHARGING IN HEAD-ON?!
HOLD IT, VIOLA! SOMETHING'S NOT RIGHT!

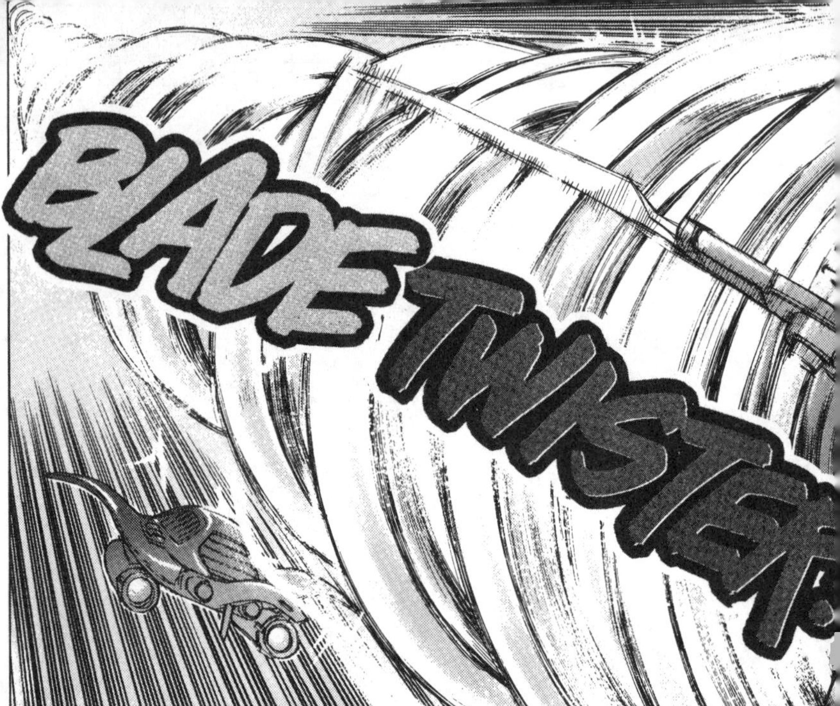
BLADE TWISTER!
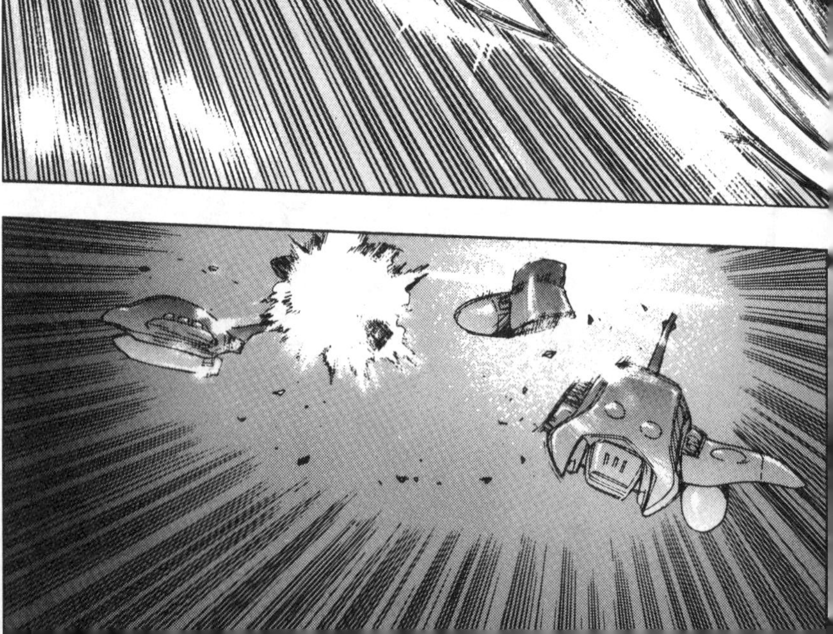

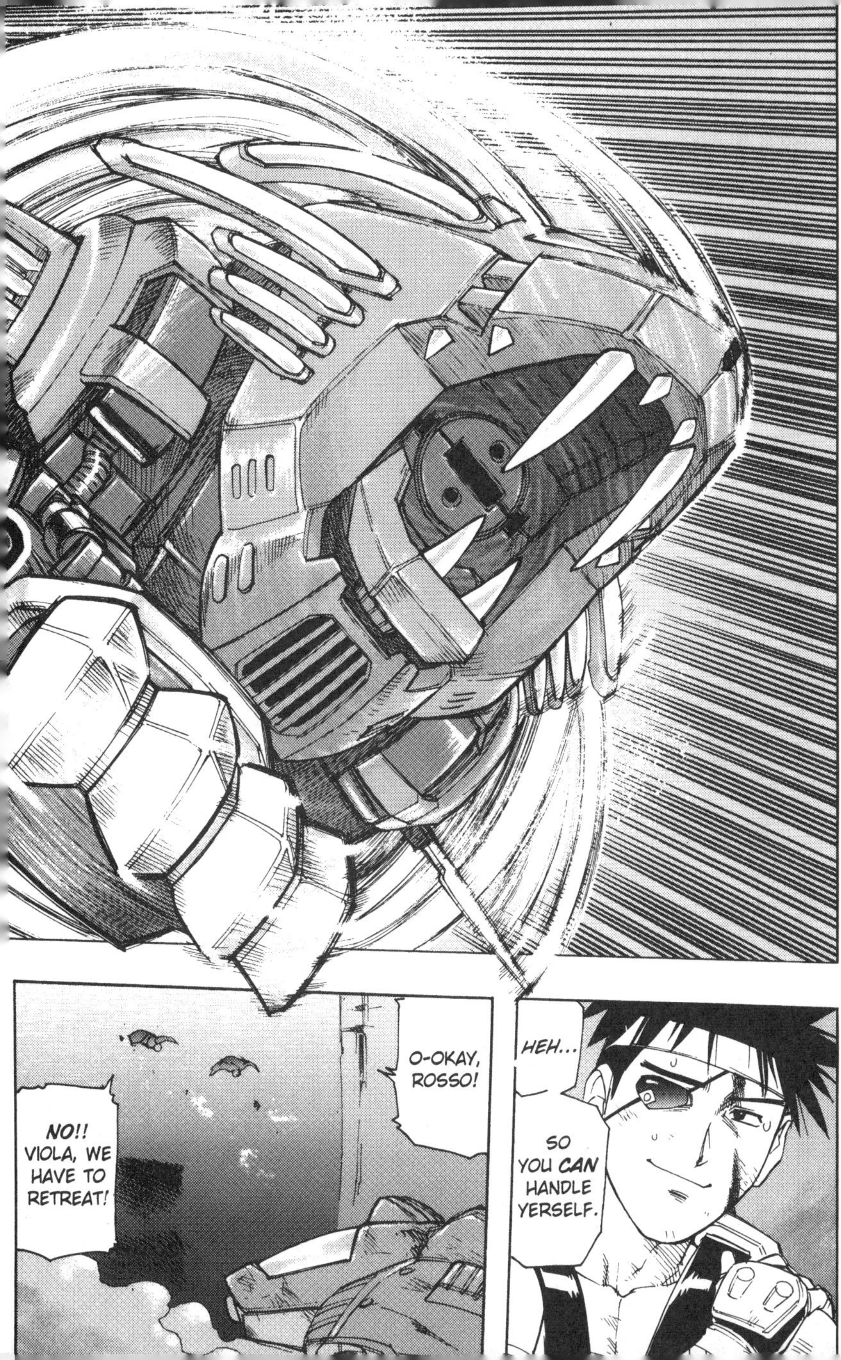
HEH...
SO YOU CAN HANDLE YERSELF.
NO!! VIOLA, WE HAVE TO RETREAT!
O-OKAY, ROSSO!

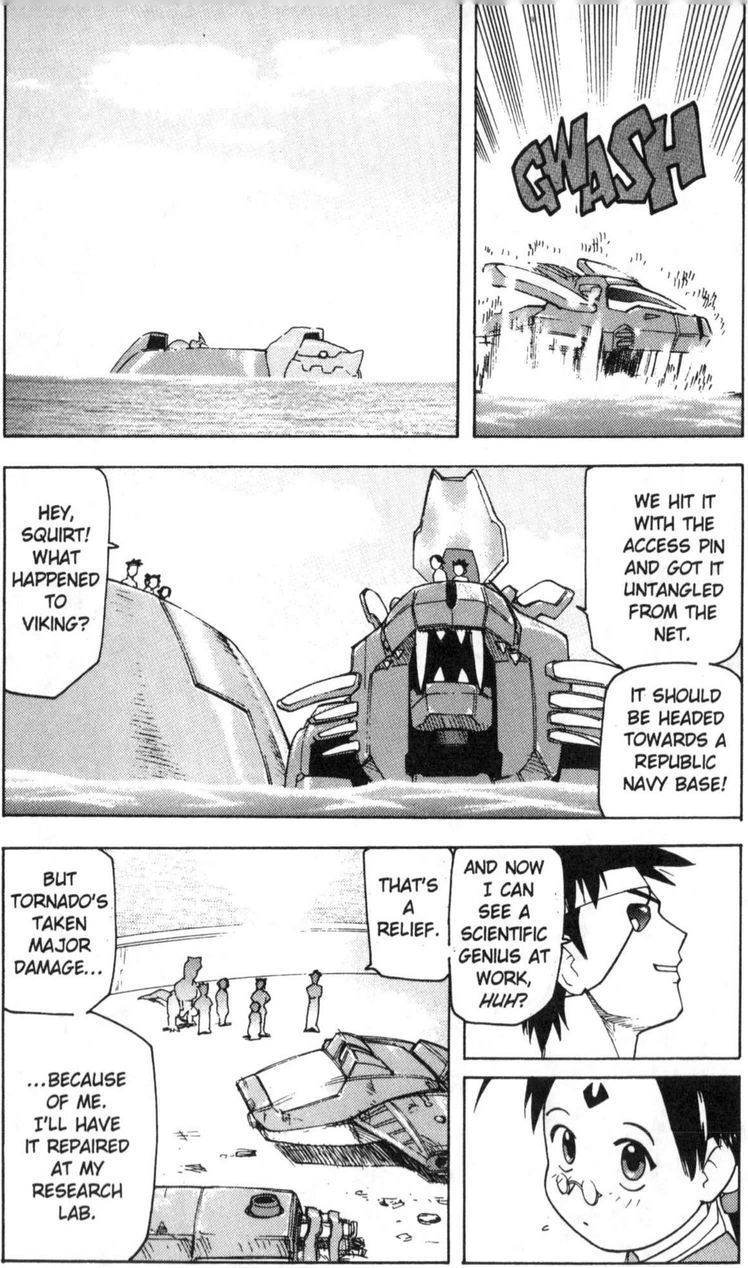
GWASH
HEY, SQUIRT! WHAT HAPPENED TO VIKING?
WE HIT IT WITH THE ACCESS PIN AND GOT IT UNTANGLED FROM THE NET.
IT SHOULD BE HEADED TOWARDS A REPUBLIC NAVY BASE!
BUT TORNADO'S TAKEN MAJOR DAMAGE...
...BECAUSE OF ME. I'LL HAVE IT REPAIRED AT MY RESEARCH LAB.
THAT'S A RELIEF.
AND NOW I CAN SEE A SCIENTIFIC GENIUS AT WORK, *HUH?*

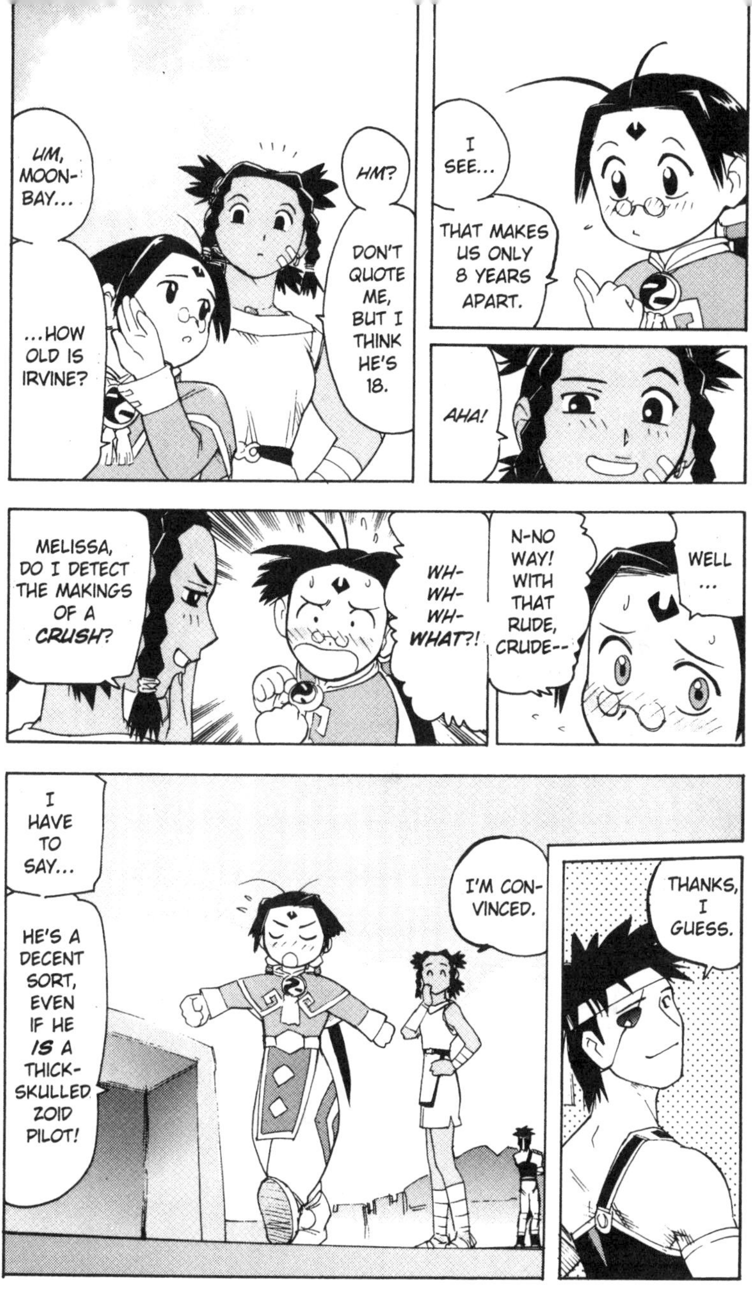
UM, MOON-BAY...
...HOW OLD IS IRVINE?
HM?
DON'T QUOTE ME, BUT I THINK HE'S 18.
I SEE...
THAT MAKES US ONLY 8 YEARS APART.
AHA!
MELISSA, DO I DETECT THE MAKINGS OF A CRUSH?
WH-WH-WH-WHAT?!
N-NO WAY! WITH THAT RUDE, CRUDE--
WELL...
I HAVE TO SAY...
HE'S A DECENT SORT, EVEN IF HE IS A THICK-SKULLED ZOID PILOT!
I'M CON-VINCED.
THANKS, I GUESS.

TO BE CONTINUED!

RZ-028 Blade Liger

Type: Lion
Length: 25.9m
Height: 12.2m
Weight: 124t
Speed: 305kph
Crew: 1~2
Equipment:
Laser Blade x2
Strike Claw x4
3D Dual Sensor
Rocket Boosters
Pulse Laser Gun x2
Laser Saber(tooth) x2
E-Shield Generator x2
Multi-Blade Antenna x2
Completion Refrigerator x4
AZ Double-Barreled Shock Cannon

Zi-025 Gustav Moonbay's Personal Zoid

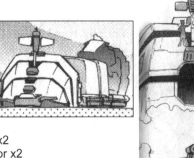

(a.k.a. RPZ-02)
Type: Insect
Length: 14.7m
Height: 9.36m
Weight: 68t
Speed: 135kph
Crew: 1
Equipment:
Traction Platform x2
Land Mine Detector x2
GPS Composite Sensor
Shock-Resistant Shell Armor
Operation Arm, Weld Arm, Refuel Tower, Carrier, Elevator Vehicle

ZOID STATISTICAL INFORMATION

EZ-026 Geno Saurer

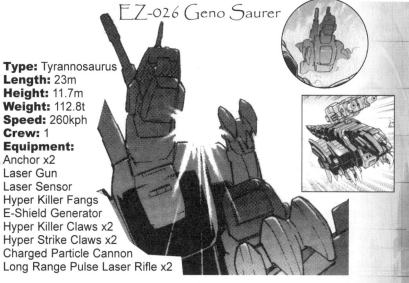

Type: Tyrannosaurus
Length: 23m
Height: 11.7m
Weight: 112.8t
Speed: 260kph
Crew: 1
Equipment:
Anchor x2
Laser Gun
Laser Sensor
Hyper Killer Fangs
E-Shield Generator
Hyper Killer Claws x2
Hyper Strike Claws x2
Charged Particle Cannon
Long Range Pulse Laser Rifle x2

EZ-032 Sinker

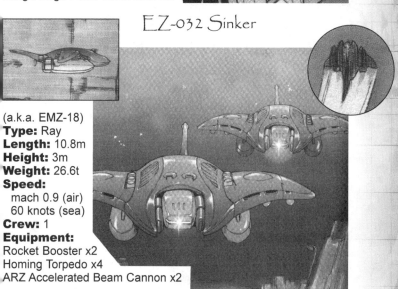

(a.k.a. EMZ-18)
Type: Ray
Length: 10.8m
Height: 3m
Weight: 26.6t
Speed:
  mach 0.9 (air)
  60 knots (sea)
Crew: 1
Equipment:
Rocket Booster x2
Homing Torpedo x4
ARZ Accelerated Beam Cannon x2

The popular robots of the Fox Kids TV series and Hasbro toy can now be found in a comic featuring two new issues every month!

From backyards, to playgrounds, to stadiums: kids and their pet robots called Medabots compete against each other in Robattles hoping ultimately to earn the title of World Robattle Champion! Medabots are robots armed with an A.I. and an impressive collection of weaponry ready to Robattle and win!

In fact, the more a Medabot battles, the more powerful it can become... and the more it stands to lose! Medabots that lose a battle yield some of their Medaparts to the winner, so every battle counts!

Medabots Comic 1 & 2
b&w...40 pages
$2.75 US and $4.50

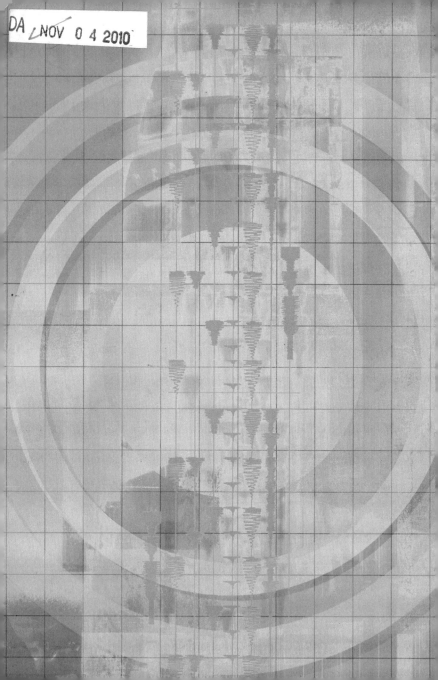